VOLUME FOURTEEN

THE E
THE PH.

"Seize him!" shouted Kali, motioning to the men who stood with him on the dock—men armed with knives and pistols. "Kill him!"

With drawn knives, the Assassins leaped on the Phantom en masse. There was a failing of fists and a chorus of grunts and groans. On Assassin fired a shot. The Phantom was bowled over backward. He twisted, cried out, and slipped into the water.

Kali folded his arms in satisfaction.

"Finish him off," he ordered.

Three Assassins dove in, knives drawn.

The water boiled and seethed.

It turned red.

Kali stroked his mustache. "Well, Ibn," he told the bald man, his monocle glinting. "That's the end of your Phantom."

Hermes Press

Published by Hermes Press, an imprint of Herman and Geer Communications, Inc.
Daniel Herman, Publisher
Troy Musguire, Production Manager
Eileen Sabrina Herman, Managing Editor
Alissa Fisher, Graphic Design
Kandice Hartner, Senior Editor
Benjamin Beers, Archivist

2100 Wilmington Road
Neshannock, Pennsylvania, 16105
(724) 652-0511
www.HermesPress.com; info@hermespress.com

Cover image: Painting of The Phantom by George Wilson
Book design by Eileen Sabrina Herman
First printing, 2020

LCCN applied for: 0 1 2 3 4 5 6 7 8 9 10
ISBN 978-1-61345-193-9
OCR and text editing by H + G Media and Eileen Sabrina Herman
Proof reading by Eileen Sabrina Herman and Kandice Hartner

From Dan, Louise, Sabrina, Ruckus, and Noodle for D'zur and Mellow

Acknowledgements: This book would not be possible without the help, cooperation, patience, and kindness of many people. First and foremost in making this endeavor a reality are Ita Golzman and Frank Caruso at King Features. Thanks also to Pete Klaus and the late Ed Rhoades of "The Friends of the Phantom." Pete and Ed have provided us with resource material, contacts, information, and helpful insights into the strip and continue to be there when we have questions about the world of The Ghost Who Walks.

Editor's Note: There were several misspellings in the original text; those have been corrected with this reprint. However, the alternate spelling for the Singh pirates as Singg was kept to preserve the original format.

Printed in Canada

AUTHORS NOTE

Old friends of the PHANTOM adventure strip may be interested to know more about this series of novels with the general title, The Story of the Phantom.

All are based on my original stories. I wrote *They Story of the Phantom—The Ghost Who Walks, The Mysterious Ambassador, Killer's Town, The Vampires and the Witch*, and this book, *The Curse of the Two-Headed Bull*.

Basil Copper adapted *The Slave Market of Mucar*, and *The Scorpia Menace*. Frank S. Shawn adapted *The Veiled Lady, The Golden Circle, The Hydra Monster, The Mystery of the Sea Horse, The Goggle-Eyes Pirates*, and *The Swamp Rats*. Warren Shanahan adapted *The Island of Dogs*, and Carson Bingham adapted *The Assassins*.

Lee Falk
1974

The Story of THE PHANTOM and The Assassins

Lee Falk

CONTENTS

WITH THE PHANTOM, EVERYTHING IS POSSIBLE— EXCEPT BOREDOM

by
Francis Lacassin, Lecturer
The Sorbonne, Paris, France

When Lee Falk introduced into comic-strip format the imaginary and the fantastic with the figure of *Mandrake, The Magician*, it was apparent that he was contributing to what I describe to my students at the Sorbonne as "The Ninth Art." It was even more evident when he invented The Phantom, a figure who set the fashion for the masked and costumed Man of Justice,

On November 5, 1971, the oldest university in Europe, the Sorbonne, opened its doors to the comics. I was privileged to give, with the section of Graphic Arts, a weekly two-hour course in the History of the Aesthetics and Language of Comic Strips. Prior sessions had been devoted to the *Phantom*. The female students were drawn to the attractiveness and elegance of his figure; the men liked his masculinity and humor. To me, Lee Falk's stories— representing as they do the present-day *Thousand and One Nights*, fairy tales, *The Tales of the Knights of the Round Table*, etc.—adapt the epic poetry for the dreams and needs of an advanced and industrial civilization. For me the Phantom reincarnates Achilles, the valorous warrior of the Trojan War, and like a knight he wanders about the world in search of a crime to castigate or a wrong to right.

Lee Falk's art of storytelling is defined as much by the succinctness of the action, as by that of the dialogue. The text has not only a dry, terse quality, but also delicious humor. The humor shows itself in the action by the choice of daring ellipses: nothing remains but the strong points of the action. This allows the story to progress more rapidly and reduces the gestures of the hero to those which underlie his fantastic physical prowess. Falk gives the drama in a nutshell. A remarkable example is the resume done in four frames (in the comic strip) and placed at the beginning of each episode to recall the Phantom's origins. In four pictures, everything about the man is said, his romantic legend, his noble mission. Moreover, the new reader enters the fabulous world of Lee Falk, where nothing is real but everything is possible—except boredom.

Dressed in a soft hat and an overcoat with the collar upturned, the Phantom and his wolf, Devil, wander about the world, the cities of Europe, or, dressed in his eighteenth-century executioner's costume, he passes his time in the jungle. Wherever he is, he acts like a sorcerer of the fantastic. Under his touch, the real seems to crack and dreams well through.

A masked ball in the Latin Quarter appears. In the Phantom's eyes it is the rendezvous of a redoubtable secret society of women. The jungle vegetation becomes the jewel box in which are hidden lost cities, sleeping gods, vampire queens, tournaments worthy of the Olympic Games. The geography, the flowers, the animals in their turn undergo a magical change brought on by the hero. A savage continent borders the edge of the Deep Woods. It is protected by a praetorian guard, the pygmies. The Skull Cave contains the treasures of war and the archives of his ancestors. All this occurs on a mythical continent which is not exactly Africa nor exactly Asia, because the tigers and lions are friends.

The genius of Lee Falk is to have known how to create a new *Odyssey*, with all of its fantastic color, but what is even more surprising is that it would be believable in the familiar settings of the modern world. The Phantom acts with the audacity of Ulysses and also with the nobility of a knight-errant. In contrast to Ulysses, and similarly to Sir Lancelot, he moves about in the world of his own free will among his peers. Lee Falk has not only managed to combine epic poetry with fairy tales and the stories of chivalry, he has made of the Phantom, in a jungle spared by colonialism, an agent of political equilibrium and friendship between races. In giving his hero an eternal mission, Lee Falk has made him so real, so near, so believable that he has made of him a man of all times. He will outlive him as Ulysses has outlived Homer. But in contrast to Ulysses, his adventures will continue after his creator is gone, because his creator has made of him an indispensable figure endowed with a life of his own. This is a privilege of which the heroes of written word cannot partake; no one has been able to imitate Homer.

However, the comic strip is the victim of a fragile medium, the newspaper. Because of this, some adventures of *The Phantom* have been lost and live only in the memory of their readers. This memory is difficult to communicate to others. Lee Falk has, therefore, given a new dimension to *The Phantom* by making of him the hero of a series of novels, introducing his origins and his first adventures to those who did not know him before.

This is not his least important accomplishment, but the most significant in my opinion is this: —in presenting to us The Phantom, as a friend, Lee Falk has taught us to dream, which is something no school in the world can teach.

Francis Lacassin
June, 1972
Paris

PROLOGUE

How It All Began

*O*ver four hundred years ago, a large British merchant ship was
*attacked by Singg pirates off the remote shores of Bangalla. The
captain of the trading vessel was a famous seafarer who, in his youth,
had served as cabin boy to Christopher Columbus on his first voyage
to discover the New World. With the captain was his son, Kit, a
strong young man who idolized his father and hoped to follow him as
a seafarer. But the pirate attack was disastrous. In a furious battle,
the entire crew of the merchant ship was killed and the ship sank in
flames. The sole survivor was young Kit who, as he fell off the burning
ship, saw his father killed by a pirate. Kit was washed ashore, half-
dead. Friendly pygmies found him and nursed him to health.*

    *One day, walking on the beach, he found a dead pirate
dressed in his fathers clothes. He realized this was the pirate who had
killed his father. Grief-stricken, he waited until vultures had stripped
the body clean. Then on the skull of his father's murderer, he swore
an oath by firelight as the pygmies watched. "I swear to devote my
life to the destruction of piracy, greed, cruelty, and injustice – and my
sons and their sons shall follow me."*

    *This was the Oath of the Skull that Kit and his descendants
would live by. In time, the pygmies led him to their home in the Deep
Woods in the center of the jungle, where he found a large cave with
many rocky chambers. The mouth of the cave, a natural formation*

formed by the water and wind of centuries, was curiously like a skull. This became his home, the Skull Cave. He soon adopted a mask and a strange costume. He found that the mystery and fear this inspired helped him in his endless battle against world-wide piracy. For he and his sons who followed became known as the nemesis of pirates everywhere, a mysterious man whose face no one ever saw, whose name no one knew, who worked alone.

As the years passed, he fought injustice wherever he found it. The first Phantom and the sons who followed found their wives in many places. One married a reigning queen, one a princess, one a beautiful red-haired barmaid. But whether queen or commoner, all followed their men back to the Deep Woods to live the strange but happy life of the wife of the Phantom. And of all the world, only she, wife of the Phantom and their children, could see his face.

Generation after generation was conceived and born, grew to manhood, and assumed the tasks of the father before him. Each wore the mask and costume. Folk of the jungle and the city and sea began to whisper that there was a man who could not die, a Phantom, a Ghost Who Walks. For they thought the Phantom was always the same man. A boy who saw the Phantom would see him again fifty years after; and he seemed the same. And he would tell his son and his grandson; and then his son and grandson would see the Phantom fifty years after that. And he would seem the same. So the legend grew. The Man Who Cannot Die. The Ghost Who Walks. The Phantom.

The Phantom did not discourage this belief in his immortality. Always working alone against tremendous – sometimes almost impossible – odds, he found that the awe and fear the legend inspired was a great help in his endless battle against evil. Only his friends, the pygmies, knew the truth. To compensate for their tiny stature, the pygmies, mixed deadly poisons for use on their weapons in hunting or defending themselves. It was rare that they were forced to defend themselves. Their deadly poisons were known through the jungle, and they and their home, the Deep Woods, were dreaded and avoided. Another reason to stay away from the Deep Woods – it soon became known that this was a home of the Phantom, and none wished to trespass.

Through the ages, the Phantoms created several more homes, or hideouts, in various parts of the world. Near the Deep Woods was the Isle of Eden, where the Phantom taught all animals to live in peace. In the southwest desert of the New World, the Phantoms created an eyrie on a high, steep mesa that was thought by the Indians to be haunted by evil spirits and became known as "Walker's Table" – for the Ghost Who Walks. In Europe, deep in the crumbling cellars of ancient castle ruins, the Phantom had another hideout from which to strike against evildoers.

But the Skull Cave in the quiet of the Deep Woods remained the true home of the Phantom. Here, in a rocky chamber, he kept his chronicles, written records of all his adventures. Phantom after Phantom faithfully recorded their experiences in the large folio volumes. Another chamber contained the costumes of all the generations of Phantoms. Other chambers contained the vast treasures of the Phantom acquired over the centuries, used only in the endless battle against evil.

Thus twenty generations of Phantoms lived, fought, and died, usually violently, as they fulfilled their oath. Jungle folk, sea folk and city folk believed him the same man, the Man Who Cannot Die. Only the pygmies knew that always, a day would come when their great friend would die. Then, alone, a strong young son would carry his father to the burial crypt of his ancestors where all Phantoms rested. As the pygmies waited outside, the young man would emerge from the cave, wearing the mask, the costume, and the skull ring of the Phantom; his carefree, happy days as the Phantom's son were over. And the pygmies would chant their age-old chant, "The Phantom is dead. Long live the Phantom."

The story of the Island of Dogs is an adventure of the Phantom of our time—the twenty-first generation of his line. He has inherited the traditions and responsibilities created by four centuries of Phantom ancestors. One ancestor created the Jungle Patrol. Thus, today, our Phantom is the mysterious and unknown commander of this elite corps. In the jungle, he is known and loved as The Keeper of the Peace. On his right hand is the Skull Ring that leaves his mark— the Sign of the Skull—known and feared by evildoers everywhere. On his left hand—closer to the heart—is his "good mark" ring. Once given, the mark grants the lucky bearer protection by the Phantom, and it is equally known and respected. And to good people and criminals alike in the jungle, on the seven seas, and in the cities of the world he is the Phantom, the Ghost Who Walks, the Man Who Cannot Die.

Lee Falk
New York 1973

CHAPTER 1

It was a clear, warm day in Bangalla, with not a cloud in the sky and ho sign of civilization's aI'mospheric pollution. The rains had come and gone for the season. The air was as heady as vintage wine.

In the middle of that remote section of the country called the Deep Woods, a tall muscular man, six-feet-six, with wide shoulders and strong legs, strode vigorously through the heavy jungle growth.

He was dressed in his traditional mask, hood and skintight costume, with belt and two handguns holstered at his waist. Although his name was Kit Walker, he was known to the good and the bad of the world as the Phantom, the Ghost Who Walks.

It was during a period of unexpected leisure that he had taken to making these long walks in the afternoon to keep himself in shape.

As he came through a stand of cocopalms near a small pool formed by an old abandoned beaver dam, he saw a movement in the undergrowth. He hesitated. Usually he did not run across the beasts of the jungle. They were quite accustomed to his comings and goings and stayed out of his way from habit.

A stray lion? A tiger on the prowl?

No.

It was a young woman sitting beside a pool, soaking her feet in the cool water.

The Phantom frowned. What kind of security was this? No one knew this stretch of the jungle but the Bandar pygmies, the "little poison people" who inhabited it. No one dared enter the area but the Phantom himself. It was dangerous for any human being who was not familiar with the beasts in residence. And forbidden to all tribes by the ancient decree of the first Phantom.

But the girl couldn't have cared less. She was blue-eyed, with red hair and freckles. Actually, she was quite pretty. The Phantom gazed at her exposed legs and found himself thinking of Diana Palmer, whom he had not seen for months. Diana was his sweetheart from his college days at Harrison University in the United States.

"Hello." The girl had a slight British accent.

The Phantom stared. She was watching him in the pool where his form was reflected on the surface of the water.

"Hello. Who are you?"

"I'm Lola Bateman." She smiled. Her freckles were not particularly unattractive, but when she smiled he was conscious of two large front teeth. "You're Kit Walker, aren't you?"

"Some call me that," said the Phantom. "I'm sorry to inform you that this is all forbidden country. You'll have to leave."

She pouted. "I say, now."

"It's very dangerous here," the Phantom insisted, becoming slightly exasperated at her stubbornness.

"I'm a very brave girl." She grinned. "Besides, you can protect me. You're the bravest man in the world."

The Phantom, unable to think of a rejoinder, bit his lip.

"Mainly I like it because it's cool. And I like to soak my feet."

"I see."

She watched him. "They say I have nice feet." She traced her finger in the dirt by her side. "Back in London."

"That's good," the Phantom observed sagely.

"Thank you." She blushed and it seemed as if she could blush at will.

"Well." The Phantom came around the pool and reached out his hand to help her to her feet. "We'll have to get you out of here, won't we?"

Her lips pushed out in a pout. "Will we? Why?"

"It's for your own safety, Lola." The Phantom reached

down gallantly to take her hand. "Deadly snakes. Lethal rodents. Killer cats. All that sort of thing."

"Oh, dear. But I'm of very good stock. I'm not frightened."

The Phantom nodded. "Excellent." He grasped her hand and lifted her quickly. She was heavier than she looked. "Upsy-daisy. On your feet."

Lola pouted at the ground. "My shoes." She pointed.

The Phantom let go of her hand and picked up her shoes. "Let's go."

"I can't walk without my shoes!"

The Phantom stared at the shoes in his hand and then at her. "But you said you were of such good stock."

She flushed with annoyance. "Are you going to insult me?"

He handed the shoes to her. "Put them on."

She stamped a foot. "You're being mean to me! You put them on."

The Phantom shook his head. He was not used to the company of people. Nor was he used to the society of coy, flirtatious women. How had this one gotten here, anyway?

"Are you going to put them on?" Lola's voice was suddenly soft and beguiling. He was conscious of the pressure of her hand on his arm.

The Phantom stooped and slipped one shoe on her foot, then the other. He could not avoid noticing her ankles and her legs. They were quite adequately formed.

"Do we have to go now?"

The Phantom stood and stared down at her. "You've got your shoes on, and you can walk. Right?"

"Yes."

"Then we have to go."

They started off through the palm stand and onto a sandy flatland. Lola switched her hips next to him, flouncing out her cotton dress. "You're not very nice, you know."

"Sorry about that. I'm a very busy man and I have little time to cultivate the social amenities."

"What do you do?"

The Phantom smiled. "I travel."

'To London?"

"Sometimes."

"Do you like me?"

The Phantom frowned. "I hardly know you."

"Perhaps we could remedy that!"

"That brings up an important question." The Phantom was trying to rein in his growing anger.

"Yes?"

"How did you get here?"

"I was invited."

"I see. And who invited you?"

"A funny little man named Guran."

The Phantom bit his lower lip. So this was Guran's doing! Wait until he got hold of the little pygmy! He'd tell him a thing or two.

"He said you'd be out walking today." Lola smiled, wrinkling her nose.

The Phantom eyed her shrewdly. "And he told you where."

"Yes. He was right, too," she added after a pause.

"About what?"

"You're a very shy person." She giggled. "Well, I can take care of that."

"You can?" The Phantom was beginning to walk faster and faster. Lola was having trouble keeping up with him.

"I certainly can. I'm not shy at all."

"That's rather obvious."

"Hey, wait!" Lola stumbled in the sand. "What's the hurry?"

"I'm late," said the Phantom over his shoulder, increasing the distance between the two of them.

"For what?"

"A public whipping."

"Who, for goodness' sake?"

"Guran."

And the Phantom was gone.

Lola Bateman was exhausted and disgusted by the time she got back to the Phantom's cave.

In a way, she was not surprised to see her luggage packed and waiting there for her return flight to London from Mawitaan, the capital of Bangalla.

When the Phantom finally coaxed Guran in out of the tall bush where he had hidden during the night, the two of them retired to the Skull Cave where the Phantom had all his books, records, and communications equipment—everything that had to do with his professional role as the twenty-first Phantom.

Guran and the Phantom together might have made an amusing picture of incompatibles to the average observer, with the Phantom at six-feet-six, towering over the pygmy, who was four-feet-four. The two had known each other all their lives. Guran had been Kit Walker's constant companion throughout his formative years, and even during part of his stay in America.

Now, Guran had reverted to native costume, with a hat woven out of cocopalm fronds and a skirt made of palm leaves belted around his fat middle. Guran was Chief of the Bandar tribe, with total responsibility for the government of the Deep Woods.

The Phantom leaned over the desk like an executive in a penthouse suite rather than a hooded man in a cave and glowered at Guran.

"That was uncalled for," he began, "and it was a sneaky thing to do besides. You know how I detest guile of any kind."

The little black pygmy was perspiring. "But Phantom, the Chiefs and I have been worried lately about your health."

"Do I seem sickly? Do I seem dispirited? Why have you been worried about me?"

"You have no woman. Everybody has a woman."

The Phantom stared at the floor of the office. "I see."

"You are not getting any younger."

"True, true." The Phantom put his hand to his chin and frowned slightly.

"If there is no progeny, Ghost Who Walks, the bloodline of the great fighter of piracy, cruelty, and injustice will die out."

"I know the facts of life."

"All of us met secretly and decided on a course of action—to bring you a woman to carry on your line."

The Phantom growled in his throat and rose to pace back and forth in front of Guran.

"Has it ever occurred to you that I might like to pick my own?"

"It occurred to us, yes."

"Then why on earth don't you let me?"

"We have been waiting a long time."

There was silence while the Phantom sank back into his chair and stared once again, this time at the ceiling.

"It is not easy for a man to select the proper mate."

Guran shrugged. "It is not easy to select an improper mate, either," said Guran. "But men do."

"You chide me because I am not a romantic fool?"

"We are worried about the family line," Guran explained steadily. "That is all. We do not disparage your remarkable achievements."

"No, no," sighed the Phantom. "Very well. I suppose you have a point."

"Indeed we do."

"Oddly enough, I was thinking of Diana Palmer today."

"Diana Palmer is in the United States."

"Yes. I knew her when I was in college."

Guran nodded. "I remember her very well."

"It is possible that I could visit her and—" The Phantom hesitated and plunged into meditation.

"And?" prompted Guran.

"And possibly—well, renew our old acquaintance." The Phantom's face heated up.

"I'll tell the Chiefs of the Jungle." Guran rose, his round face sparkling with suppressed mirth and joy.

"Don't tell them yet."

"You won't break your word, Ghost Who Walks?"

"No. No. I'll pack today. I'll fly to the States from the capital tomorrow!"

Guran hurried out. "I'll take care of the airline tickets!"

The Phantom sank back in his chair. "I thought you would."

CHAPTER 2

At approximately the same moment that the Phantom boarded a jetliner bound for America in the Bangalla capital, Diana Palmer was standing on a jetty about to board a four-engined seaplane bound for remote Bangalla. With her were her mother and her Uncle Dave.

A scattering of passengers were moving about on the jetty, waiting for boarding time. The amphibian would be fairly full, but not crowded.

"I just hope you're doing the right thing." Diana's mother began fussing with the traveling bag to make sure it would not snap open.

"Yes, Mother," Diana responded dutifully.

Diana was a dark-haired, dark-eyed, very beautiful girl with an outdoorsy, healthy look. She was in her early twenties, a lively person who was great fun to be with.

Her mother was stocky and plump, and she tended to be overly protective of her only daughter. She wore her gray hair in a bun under a smart hat and covered her blue eyes with large wire-rimmed glasses. She was extremely rich, because of the Palmer fortune, although she looked so plain that she might have been the family cook.

"I don't like to lecture," she continued, "but I do want to let you know what I'm thinking."

Diana smiled. Her mother always wanted to let her know what she was thinking.

"I could be wrong, but I do feel you're making a mistake wasting your time with this strange man."

"I've heard that before, Mother."

"Anyone who lives in a cave and only writes a letter once a year can't be too enthralled with you!"

"Mother, please. Kit's been busy. I'm sure he's meant to."

"I think it's nonsense, that's what I think. Why you waste your time—"

"It's her time," Uncle Dave cut in, smiling. David Palmer was a husky middle-aged man with an open face, a long nose, bright eyes, and a pipe which he continually chewed on even when it was not lit. He affected a sharply creased fedora over his steel-gray hair.

"I realize it's her time, but she's not getting any younger, you know. Certainly there are all kinds of men in our social stratum who'd love to marry her. She simply won't let any of them get close enough to her to ask."

"Mother," said Diana softly. "Please."

"Look, Diana," Uncle Dave said forcefully. "Be sure to have a good time, and give my best to your—uh, friend. I always thought he was a very intelligent and interesting fellow."

Diana laughed. "Yes, Uncle Dave."

"Funny place to board a plane, don't you think?" Uncle Dave stared out into the water at the four-engined amphibian floating beside the loading jetty. "I thought they only sent jetliners overseas today."

"No, Uncle Dave. I thought I'd take this line because it would be restful. You know, there's so much fuss and feathers aboard a regular jet. Drinks. Movies. I thought I'd just rest and maybe read a little."

"Uh. Well, the ship looks sturdy, and surprisingly enough, there are quite a few people taking it."

"I think they're tired of those infernal, time-consuming checkouts at the big airports," Mrs. Palmer said. "It's enough to provoke a saint. As if anyone would try to hijack a plane these days!"

"They do, though," Uncle Dave frowned.

"I'll be perfectly fine." Diana stooped over to pick up her carryall. "I think they're getting ready to board."

Uncle Dave put out his hand. "Have a safe trip, Diana. And enjoy yourself!"

"Thanks, Uncle Dave. I will."

Diana's mother presented her cheek for a kiss, and Diana obliged. "Take care of yourself. And watch out for that— that man."

"I will. Mother."

Diana moved over and stood in line as a uniformed steward opened the door of the ship and stepped down to prop it against the side of the airplane. The passengers slowly filed in, showing their boarding slips to the stewardess at the door.

Diana's mother was watching with Uncle Dave. "Would you look at that distinguished man? Isn't he something? I wish Diana would fall for someone like that, instead of that strange creature she's going to see."

Uncle Dave glanced at the man his sister-in-law had pointed out. The man in question was tall and erect, middle-aged, and dressed with a sartorial perfection that hinted at a continental tailor. He wore a pearl-gray hat, a limp blue polka-dot scarf that was knotted loosely over his throat, and an expensive suit, cut in the European style. There was a monocle in his right eye and a waxed mustache above his flat lips. He smoked a cigarette in an elaborate holder. If anything, he seemed to be a fashion plate about fifteen years out of date.

"Maybe Diana doesn't like monocles." Uncle Dave didn't like them himself.

"Humph." Diana's mother turned up her nose. "You're just like all the rest of them, aren't you?"

The tall man with the monocle glanced around hurriedly and made a slight motion of the hand as if to signal someone. Uncle Dave could not see for whom the signal was intended. Then, as he pondered, he realized there were two heavily built men, each dressed in nondescript gray suits, who were boarding the plane just in back of Diana. The signal was apparently directed at one of them.

Odd.

"Well, I suppose we'd better walk back to the car," said Mrs. Palmer as Diana stepped into the plane, turning at the last moment to wave at them.

Uncle Dave nodded, still curious about the odd signal he had seen.

Diana moved along the aisle and found a seat by a window. She put her carryall in the rack above the seat and settled down to fasten the safety belt around her waist.

She was excited because she had been thinking about the Phantom for months. It was simply because her mother had become so insistent that she go out with other young men— "beaux" as she called them—that Diana had decided to visit the

Phantom.

It was disappointing, of course, that none of her letters to him had been answered promptly. Of course, she knew that the Phantom spent most of his time on mysterious business engagements all over the world. But still, he could write to her more often.

Of course, most men do not correspond the way women do. She settled down and peered through the porthole. She was on the side of the ship opposite the dock and could not see her mother and uncle. Soon she was conscious of a strange scent wafting through the air.

She turned.

In the aisle by her seat was a middle-aged man apparently totally inundated by an after-shave lotion or cologne with a spicy, almost citrus-like, odor. He wore a waxed mustache, a monocle, and he was now removing his scarf and suit coat. He smiled at her as he placed them in the rack above the seat.

"I don't mean to intrude, but is this seat available?" He made a slight and rather effeminate bow.

Diana shrugged. "Yes, it is." She turned to the porthole. She hoped it wasn't going to be one of those talk-talk flights. She wanted to rest and read and think.

"Thank you." The man sank into the seat, rapidly adjusting the seat belt.

A moment later, the pilot shut the door to the cockpit, the steward closed the loading port with a slam, and the engines started.

Ten minutes later they were airborne.

"It isn't often one sits next to such a charming companion." The mustached man began talking as soon as the no smoking lights were off. "Do you mind if I smoke? And would you like one yourself?"

Diana hesitated. It would be rude to say that she hated the smell of smoke and that she objected to tobacco for ecological reasons. She was too polite for that. "Not at all." She smiled faintly. "And, no thank you. I don't want one myself."

"Never took it up," the mustached man observed with a bright laugh.

Diana tried to place the accent. The man's speech was not guttural enough to be German, and it was not nasal enough to be French. Hungarian? No. Russian? Possibly. Greek? It was difficult to tell. Diana was no expert on accents. She didn't even care about his voice. It was enough that the man's cologne was overpowering.

"You're a remarkably beautiful woman." He placed a

cigarette in an elaborate ivory holder and lighted up. "Most Americans are not beautiful, as I see it. But you are, Miss . . . ?"

"Miss Palmer." Diana sighed and turned from the window.

"Yes, Miss Palmer. I am Henry Kali. It is a pleasure to make your acquaintance. Tell me, was that lovely couple you were talking with on the dock your parents?"

"No."

Kali started, looking abashed.

"One was my mother. The other was my uncle."

"I see." Kali smiled. "There's good in those people. America is a fine land, a proud country."

"Yes."

"I am a citizen of the world. Miss Palmer. That is, I do not dwell exclusively in one country. I have business connections everywhere, and therefore, I maintain residences in most capital cities."

"How nice," said Diana.

"That is why I travel so much. It is required by my international profession."

"Oh."

Kali continued to drone on, flicking his finger against the cigarette and splashing the ashes onto the carpeting, adjusting his monocle every so often, grinning at her, running his hand through his greasy black hair, and emanating that overpowering cologne.

Diana tried to shut out the sound and smell, but she could not.

He was still talking during the meal. Once he stood up and peered past Diana's shoulder out the porthole and then settled himself again in his seat.

When the stewardess came to take away the empty coffee cups, Diana glanced out the porthole and was surprised to see lights on the surface of the water far below.

"Do you think that is a fishing boat?" she asked, pointing it out to Kali.

Kali leaned over her and smiled. "I do believe it is, Miss Palmer."

"Isn't it quite far at sea? I thought fishing boats usually stayed reasonably close to shore."

"Indeed they do." Kali glanced at his wristwatch. "Right on time."

"I beg your pardon?"

"Nothing." Kali stood abruptly. "Will you excuse me, Miss Palmer?"

"Certainly."

Out of the corner of her eye, she saw Kali walk down the

aisle of the plane toward the cockpit. As he passed the seat ahead of her, she saw him reach out and touch the shoulder of the man seated there. Although she could not hear him, she knew he said something.

That was curious, she thought.

She watched as Kali approached the stewardess who had served them dinner. He pointed to the door of the cockpit and seemed to be asking the stewardess if he could go inside. The stewardess shook her head. Then Diana saw Kali remove money from his wallet and give it to the stewardess.

A moment later he was walking into the cockpit.

Even more curious, thought Diana. Kali did not strike her as the type of man who was interested enough in aviation to pay his way for a look into the cockpit of a plane.

There was a sudden lurch as the ship faltered, tilted, and then regained its stability.

From the cockpit came a muffled sound of gunfire.

Diana half rose from her seat, hand to her open mouth.

Ahead of her the man whom Kali had touched on the shoulder leaped into the aisle of the plane, moved quickly to the cockpit door, and turned to face the passengers. At the same time, he slipped his hand into his jacket pocket and removed a gun.

"Ladies and gentlemen," he snapped, "you will remain seated, please!"

Skyjackers, thought Diana. And Kali was their leader!

CHAPTER 3

When the cockpit door opened, Captain Harmon, pilot of the airliner, had turned around expecting to see the stewardess with coffee for him and Lieutenant Anders, his co-pilot. Instead, he saw a tall man with a monocle and slicked-back hair.

"Yes, sir?"

The door closed immediately. The intruder reached inside his suit and pulled out a revolver which he aimed at Harmon's head.

"This is the end of the line, Captain Harmon. I'm taking over."

Harmon snorted. "Who are you, and what are you up to? We're in mid-ocean!"

"Exactly why I boarded a seaplane." The man smiled flatly. "Now don't give me any trouble."

Lieutenant Anders was speaking into a microphone. "Mayday, Ground Control. Mayday. Latitude—"

The gun in the intruder's hand fired instantly. The slug tore apart the radio in the center of the instrument panel.

"Enough of that," snapped the skyjacker. "Now do as I say, or I'll kill the first one who makes a false move."

"You're crazy," said Harmon. "You can't get away with this!"

"Oh, I'll get away with it, all right. Now let's put the plane down."

"We're miles from land!" Harmon protested.

"We passed a small fishing boat one minute ago. Circle, and land near it."

"You must be out of your mind!" cried Anders.

The gun fired again. The slug smashed into the wall of the cockpit.

"A warning," the man chuckled softly. "The next shot will not miss. Do as I say!"

There was silence. The ship started down.

Trying not to allow her fear to overcome her, Diana Palmer watched the ocean as the plane descended to meet it. Although it was dark, lights from the lone fishing vessel illuminated the water for hundreds of yards.

The large four-engined seaplane landed in the water and coasted to a stop.

In front of Diana, a large portly passenger in a baggy suit stood up and waved his fist in the air.

"I won't stand for this!" he shouted. I'm on an important business trip! A delay could mean millions to my company!"

"Simmer down, pops." The armed man standing in front of the cockpit door glowered at the big passenger. "Sit down before I blow you into your seat."

Another man stood at the rear of the plane, training a gun on the passengers from the other direction. He was as hard-faced as the man in front of the cockpit door.

The cockpit door opened and Kali stepped out, smiling behind his monocle.

"You must excuse us for the unscheduled stop, ladies and gentlemen. You will all be well taken care of. There is no need to panic. The captain has agreed to cooperate, so no life has been expended superfluously."

"See here!" snapped the portly man, about to rise again.

"Please do not descend to histrionics, sir," cautioned Kali. "Now, stewardess, please open the passenger loading door."

The stewardess, hands trembling, complied, and the door opened outwardly. Through the opening, Diana could see the fishing boat with two men, stripped to the waist, standing on the deck. The seamen wore turbans around their heads.

"Good," said Kali, smiling benevolently at the passengers. "Now, if you'll all be kind enough to file out onto the gangplank which the seamen are fastening to the plane, no one will be harmed."

Diana glanced around. This was not the usual type of skyjack, when someone took over a plane and ordered the pilot to fly him to Cuba or Algeria. Nor was it the ransom type, with the skyjacker demanding a million dollars for safe delivery of the passengers. Kali evidently wanted the plane and that was all. Odd.

The passengers had begun straggling toward the door, some

grumbling, but mostly numbed with shock and panic-stricken. One by one they stumbled down the aisle, turned, and clattered over the gangplank which was held in place by the two grinning sailors.

Diana moved out into the aisle and joined the line of passengers. At that moment she felt a hand on her shoulder.

"Not you, Miss Palmer. You're coming with us."

Diana was stunned. Kali was smiling at her through the monocle, his fingers digging into her arm.

"I most certainly am not!" cried Diana.

"Yes, you are." Kali's grip tightened, and he pulled her from the line of people. The passengers watched her apathetically and continued to go out through the door.

Diana fought back. Kali's face turned grim. He dragged her to the front of the cabin and forced her into the seat. "You stay there!"

"No, I won't!" Diana jumped up.

At that moment the rear door slammed shut. She could see the two husky seamen standing in the aisle by the second gunman.

Kali laughed. "I'm afraid it's quite a swim, Miss Palmer!"

He crossed to the porthole and stood looking down at the passengers and crew on the fishing boat.

"Good-bye, ladies and gentlemen! I'm afraid I lied a bit to you. Your fishing boat is rudderless and without radio or engine."

There were shouts of anger from the vessel.

"But don't worry, you won't drift long."

Diana felt a chill up and down her backbone.

Kali smiled. "I've left a time bomb aboard the boat!"

A woman shrieked.

"Don't bother to look for it," Kali continued. "It's very well hidden. And it's timed to go off in exactly five minutes—long before you could locate it. *Au revoir.*" Kali closed the porthole.

Diana jumped from her seat. "You monster!" she screamed.

She ran down the aisle and thrust herself at the closed door. One of the heavily muscled seamen reached out to take her arm.

She twisted away. In her panic, she looked up and down the aisle and saw only Kali and his gunmen. Then, almost within reach, she saw a section of the ship's hull labeled EMERGENCY EXIT.

She grabbed at the handle, twisted, and the entire section fell open.

"Grab her!" yelled Kali.

One of the seamen jumped toward her, but she threw herself past him out into space. The shock of the cold sea water almost knocked the breath out of her, but she was an excellent swimmer and she struck out for the boat not more than ten yards away.

On the deck the passengers were crowded at the rail watching her. One of the men held out his hand.

Before she could cover the distance between herself and the

vessel, she felt another splash nearby and saw the grim face of the second gunman churning toward her, his powerful arms propelling him swiftly through the water.

He grabbed her.

"I've got her!" he yelled to Kali.

"Good!" growled Kali's voice from above.

She felt herself immobilized by the gunman's strong arms. Through the air a rope was flung down from the airplane.

The gunman tied a quick knot, looped it under Diana's arms.

"Stop it!" she cried. "You're hurting me."

She fought desperately to get out of the loop, but almost immediately she felt herself being lifted out of the water and hauled up toward the emergency exit of the plane.

On board the fishing boat, someone shouted to her, "I'll help you!"

Instantly there was a gunshot from above her, and the voice screamed in pain.

Diana knew there would be no more help from that quarter.

The rope tightened on her body as she was hauled unceremoniously aboard through the escape hatch she had activated.

Wet and shivering, she was untied and pushed into one of the seats as the deckhands closed the exit.

"Look out there, Miss Palmer." Kali gestured with a smile. Diana peered out the porthole at the boat. "Well?"

"Say good-bye to them, if you wish."

"You're a cold-blooded murderer! Leaving a bomb on that ship!"

"Perhaps," said Kali with a faint smile.

"You're the most despicable man I've ever met!" Diana could hear the engines of the airplane throbbing. "Are you a pilot?"

Kali shood his head, and reached into his pocket for a cigarette to insert in his holder. "No. But my two men are. You have nothing to fear, my dear."

"And don't call me 'my dear'!"

Kali shrugged. "If you insist."

"Just why did you decide to take me along with you?"

The plane began to move through the water for takeoff. "Don't flatter yourself by thinking it was your personality and intelligence, Miss Palmer," Kali said in sardonic tones. "It was purely a matter of money. I'm most interested in your bank account."

"My bank account?"

"Yes. The bank account of the famous explorer and heiress, Miss Diana Palmer."

"Where are you taking me?"

Kali smiled faintly. "You'll soon learn your destination. Don't worry about it."

Diana clenched her fists in frustration. "What do you intend to do with me?"

"Actually, I studied the passenger list ahead of time, and I made the decision not too long before we were to board the plane. It was a toss-up between you and Arnold Jenson, the international financier."

Diana frowned. "That must have been the big man who was so annoyed at the skyjacking."

"He has reason to be. But anyway, I decided that you would be easier to hold for ransom than he. And so I chose you."

"You mean you set up this whole thing just to kidnap me?" Kali shook his head slowly. "Not precisely, my dear. Mainly, we wanted the plane. You are, actually—how shall I put it?—an extra dividend."

Diana stared at Kali grimly, and then shook her head and sank her face into her hands. She knew that there was nothing she could do now. She would have to wait until they got to their destination—wherever that was.

Kali puffed on his cigarette and wandered into the cockpit to speak to his pilots.

Diana sank back and closed her eyes in bitter frustration.

CHAPTER 4

With a great deal of suppressed emotion, Captain Harmon stood by the railing of the small fishing boat and stared into the dark sky where the lights of the plane he had been flying were now disappearing into the distance.

There would be an inquiry and, quite possibly, a great deal of company flak over the skyjacking. Their flights were short, except for the Bangalla run, and they had not been subject to the same kind of extortion and violence as the major airlines.

"It's a nightmare!" a voice growled next to him. "They can't do this to us!"

Harmon turned and tried to smile. He knew the man at his side was Arnold Jenson, an international financier. "But they have, Mr. Jenson."

"Well, it's all your fault. You shouldn't have let them get us out of that plane!"

"They were armed, and we are not allowed to carry arms, sir." Harmon tried to keep his tone steady. He had reservations about the rules of the airlines, and it was difficult to hide his own belief in a tougher policy, but he had to in order to keep his job.

"Bushwah!" snorted the big portly man. "You could have shown a little muscle. They'd have caved in."

"Not likely. They worked out a very good scheme. The

fishing boat waiting which made the takeover possible. Frankly, we just aren't used to the kind of skyjacking you get on the big jetliners."

"It's a bad situation, and I intend to make a great deal of noise about it, Captain."

"You're welcome to," Harmon rejoined. "If we get back to the States, of course."

Jenson's eyes widened. "My God! You don't think that monster really has a bomb secreted aboard this craft, do you?"

"He was pretty definite about it." Lieutenant Anders had strolled up during the conversation between Harmon and Jenson.

"Well then," said Jenson, "don't you think we had all better tear this ship apart until we find it?"

"The steward and stewardesses have been doing just that," Harmon said. "I'm inclined to think the skyjacker was bluffing."

Jenson moved away from the railing. "I'm going to take a look for myself. I don't trust any of the namby-pamby personnel you have working for you."

Harmon exchanged a glance with Anders. "Mr. Jenson is a bit upset about the situation, Anders."

"Aren't you?"

"Sure. But I'm paid not to show it."

Anders grinned. "Let's get moving, Dan. Maybe we can locate that bomb."

Harmon raised an eyebrow. "Possibly."

The steward stripped off his shirt and trousers and dove into the water, swimming around the hull of the vessel. He surfaced finally and called up:

"I've been all around the boat, Captain. I can't see anything on the hull."

"Right," said Harmon. He glanced at his watch. "Only three minutes to go."

The tempo of the search sped up, and Jenson hastily opened all the crates and barrels in the hold but discovered only a modicum of food supplies.

No bomb.

Harmon was moving quickly through the cabins to make sure no area was missed.

The second hand on his watch continued its relentless sweep around the face.

Twenty seconds to go.

Thirteen.

Four.

One.

Without incident the jetliner carrying the Phantom landed at the airport outside the city in which Diana Palmer lived. The Phantom was dressed in the costume he usually wore when in the presence of civilized people—pulled-down hat, dark sunglasses, and belted trenchcoat. He took a taxi to the city and registered at a hotel for the night. He would go to Diana's in the morning.

At a newsstand in the hotel he read the headlines:

AIRCRAFT LOST AT SEA

37 Passengers, Crew of 6 Feared Lost in Midocean

PLANES SEARCH AREA

The Phantom frowned. He had been at the porthole of the jet when they had passed a plane on the way over. He wondered curiously if it was the one that had vanished.

He took the paper to his room and read it more carefully. Actually, there was not much information in the story at all. Radio contact had been lost when the liner, one of Union Airlines' fleet of amphibians, reached the middle of the ocean.

After contact was lost, there was nothing else for anyone to go on. The passenger list had been impounded by the authorities, and the airline was now notifying relatives of the missing passengers.

The Phantom rose in the early morning, ate a hearty breakfast, and took a cab out to the Palmer house in the suburbs.

He tipped the driver and strode up the white steps to the front porch of the large old-fashioned house. A moment later he faced David Palmer, Diana's uncle.

"Hello, Mr. Palmer," the Phantom smiled, holding out his hand.

Uncle Dave, looking tired and old, blinked and smiled, then removed the pipe from his mouth. "It's Kit Walker!" he said in pleased surprise. "Dorothy! Come here! It's our old friend."

The Phantom smiled and waited for Diana's mother to appear. When she approached he was surprised to see that her eyes were red from crying and her hands were shaking.

"What's wrong?" the Phantom said.

Palmer stared. "But I thought you knew. I had no idea you didn't. Otherwise, why did you come?"

"I am at a loss." The Phantom searched Palmer's face and then turned to Mrs. Palmer. "What on earth is it?"

"It's—it's Diana!"

"What about her?"

"She's lost at sea in that plane crash!"

The Phantom stared. "You mean she was on the plane that vanished?"

"Yes," said Palmer. "And there's no news of it yet. It must have simply fallen out of the sky."

The Phantom stepped back, numbed with shock. No wonder Diana's family were upset. Diana, in that plane!

"I thought you knew about it and had come to hunt for her," said Uncle Dave hopefully.

The Phantom cleared his throat. "I certainly didn't know about it, but I'll do the best I can."

"Good."

Diana's mother straightened up and smiled faintly. "Well, we certainly don't want to keep you standing outside. Do come in. I'll get you some breakfast."

"But I've already eaten, Mrs. Palmer."

"Nonsense! That was hotel food. I'm sure you want a good healthy country breakfast."

The Phantom allowed himself to be dragged into the house with a minimum of protest. He was secretly longing for one of Mrs. Palmer's marvelous breakfasts.

After he had eaten again, the Phantom drew Diana's mother into a discussion of the plane trip.

"Where was Diana going?"

"To see you."

"To Bangalla?"

"Yes. She said she hadn't heard from you and wanted to visit you."

"I see."

"And you? What brought you to America?"

The Phantom flushed. "I wanted to see Diana."

Diana's mother's eyes widened. "Why?"

"Because we're old friends. I—I simply wanted to be sure that everything was all right." The Phantom smiled nervously.

Mrs. Palmer's eyes seemed to sparkle. "You came over to see her because you missed her, didn't you?"

"Possibly." The Phantom blinked. "But that's not getting us any nearer to finding her, is it?"

"No."

The Phantom reached for the phone. "I'm going to call the authorities at the airport to see if the plane has been found."

It took the Phantom longer than he had thought it would to contact the man in charge of the air search for the missing ship. He was Federal Aviation Agency Inspector Blount.

"Who is this?" asked Blount impatiently.

"I'm the—the fiancé of one of the passengers," said the Phantom. "I'm anxious to know if you've found out anything about the crash."

"Crash?" Blount repeated. "Who said anything about a crash?"

"I assumed the plane had vanished into the ocean, of course."

"We have no evidence to that effect," Blount replied testily.

"Then you have evidence that the ship is all right?"

"I didn't say that," Blount shouted. "We just don't think the ship went down."

"Then where is it?"

"That's what we're trying to discover," Blount explained. "It was sighted still flying some hundred miles from the spot where the ship lost radio contact."

"Ah?"

"But we haven't been able to verify it. However, as soon as we do—"

"Thank you," said the Phantom.

"Hold it," said Blount. "I'm getting a call on another phone. Will you hang on?"

"Yes."

In a minute Blount came back on. His voice was excited. "Look, we've just had a flash from one of the search planes. All the passengers with the exception of four are on a fishing boat."

"I'm looking for Miss Diana Palmer."

There was a pause while Blount was searching through a list in his hands. "I'm sorry, Miss Palmer went with the skyjackers."

"Skyjackers!" the Phantom repeated in surprise.

"Yes. The ship was taken over by sky pirates and flown away after the passengers were loaded onto a boat."

"But, Miss Palmer—"

"She left with the skyjackers. The skyjackers are listed on the passenger manifest as Henry Kali, Manly Doyle and Horace Rudd."

"But—"

"Some of the passengers think Miss Palmer was kidnapped and is being held for ransom."

"Good Lord!"

"Yes. Well, that's all the information I can give you now. The search planes have picked up the survivors, and they are being flown back here. Perhaps you'd like to speak to them later."

Uncle Dave and Mrs. Palmer were standing there with pale

faces when the Phantom hung up.

"You heard?"

They said nothing.

"Diana's been kidnapped. She's being held for ransom."

CHAPTER 5

In a makeshift interrogation room set up in the customs shed at the city airport, Captain Harmon and Lieutenant Anders supervised the comforting of the passengers before turning their attention to Federal Aviation Agency Inspector Roger Blount.

"Was your flight in satisfactory?" Blount asked with a faint smile.

Harmon grimaced. "Better than the one out, sir."

Blount chuckled. He was a large man, with blue eyes and black hair. He had the appearance of an ex-policeman, which he was, but he had gained an executive directness and authority about him from all the years spent in the investigative end of the aviation business.

"Well, now. Shall we sit down over here out of the way of the others?"

Blount referred to the reporters and television camera crews who were interviewing the passengers at the other end of the big shed. Arnold Jenson seemed to be the center of all media activity, waving his arms and gesticulating in front of the cameras and slapping his fist into his palm to emphasize his points.

The three of them settled down by a wooden field desk which had been set up by the wall.

Blount opened a tape recorder and plugged it into an outlet

in the wall.

"This is informal, you understand, but will be used as a basis for the investigation to be held later."

"Yes, sir," said Harmon.

"Right," Anders added.

"We've already got your verbal reports over the air on the rescue plane. We know all the details of the skyjacking itself. Now I'd like to go over some small points."

Harmon glanced at Anders. "Go ahead, sir."

"First of all, I don't want you to feel that you are being hounded, Captain Harmon. We are simply trying to get to the bottom of the entire episode. I hope you'll take this interrogation in that light."

"Yes, sir." Harmon tried to sit up straight. He was exhausted from the ordeal he had been through.

"It won't take long," Blount said kindly. "Now, then. This Henry Kali. We've made a trace on him, but we haven't been able to locate anyone by that name at the address given. We assume the name is a false one."

"I wouldn't know about that, sir."

"The same is true of the other two men, Manly Doyle and Horace Rudd."

"They were tough-looking characters," Anders volunteered.

"All three?"

"Well, no," said Harmon. "Kali was a fashion plate, years out of style. Mustache, monocle, cigarette holder, slicked- back black hair. He had some kind of accent, but I couldn't quite place it. Could you, Steve?" He turned to Anders.

Anders shook his head. "Not German or French. Didn't seem Scandinavian. I couldn't make it out."

"Did the two other men speak much?"

"Not enough to make out their origins. Kali was the talker and, obviously, the leader."

"That's just about what we expected." Blount frowned thoughtfully. "All right. We have our men going over the fishing boat. You say there was a bomb threat?"

Harmon cleared his throat. "Not exactly a bomb threat, sir. When the airliner was about to take off, this Henry Kali leaned out the open porthole and told us that there was a time bomb aboard the boat and that it would go off in exactly five minutes."

"I see," said Blount. "Rather a sadistic joke, wasn't it?"

"If the bomb never did exist, I'd have to say yes. If, on the other hand, the bomb was there and malfunctioned, then I'd say he was simply warning us."

"But five minutes isn't enough time to find and defuse a bomb," Blount protested.

"Yes. I thought of that." Harmon frowned. "Well, I really don't know why he did it. As you say, it must have been a twisted sense of humor."

Blount stared at the tape recorder a moment. "Unless, of course, he wanted to take your mind off the airliner itself."

"I beg your pardon?"

"I mean, in the darkness, you would have been watching it more closely if you hadn't had your minds on the time bomb aboard, wouldn't you?"

Harmon's eyes widened. "I suppose so, sir. What exactly do you mean?"

"I'm simply proposing theories, Captain. Now, in your first debriefing, you stated that the airliner took off and circled around to continue in a southeasterly direction."

"Yes. About one zero nine degrees, wouldn't you say, Steve?"

Anders nodded.

"Then it did continue on a direct course—as far as you remember?"

"We were occupied with the bomb search, of course. It really vanished very quickly, you know."

"But it didn't veer from that course during the time you had it in sight?"

"No, sir. I see what you're getting at. You think it might have been a feint. Headed southeast for a spell, and then turned northeast, or whatever?"

"It's just a thought."

Harmon shrugged. "No way of telling, is there?"

"Not really." Blount took a deep breath. "So much for the bomb that either didn't exist or didn't go off. Now. I have mentioned three of the four people who left on the airliner. Three A.K.A.'s, three aliases."

"Yes, sir."

"We have records of Miss Diana Palmer. She's a well-known heiress and explorer, among other things. A very active woman. Unspotted reputation."

"A very pretty girl, too," Harmon said gallantly.

"Well, the point is," Blount chose his words slowly, "we're trying to find out exactly why she went off with the skyjackers. Do you think she was in it with them?"

Harmon frowned. "No way. Steve and I were talking about that on the way back, we think Kali knew who she was and grabbed her as a kind of hostage in case he had any trouble."

Anders nodded. "Or else he was trying to kidnap her in the first place, and took the ship as part of the plot."

"Both possibilities had, of course, occurred to us. But there's always the chance."

"You mean maybe she was in it with them from the beginning? An accomplice?" Harmon was incredulous.

"Yes," said Blount.

"What would be the purpose? The three men had everything under control. Miss Palmer had no gun."

"But still, it does seem strange, doesn't it, that she should go along with them?"

"She tried to escape," Harmon said. "She jumped out the escape hatch on her own and swam for the fishing boat."

"One of the skyjackers jumped in after her and hauled her back on board the airliner."

Blount nodded. "It could have been an act."

"An act?" Harmon frowned. "Possibly. But what would be her purpose?"

"That's what we're wondering." Blount sighed. "Well, suppose we leave it at that, gentlemen. As I said, this is an informal debriefing. We'll have the formal interrogation later on."

After leaving the makeshift interrogation room, Blount took a taxicab out to the Palmer residence in the suburbs. The door was opened by an erect man with a pipe in his mouth.

"I'm Inspector Blount of the Federal Aviation Agency," Blount told him. "I'd like to speak to Mr. Palmer, please."

"I'm Miss Palmer's uncle," said Dave. "If you'd like to speak to Mrs. Palmer, she's here. Mr. Palmer is dead."

"Sorry," said Blount. "May I come in?"

"Certainly."

They went into the living room, which was spacious, with priceless paintings on the walls and a large Oriental rug on the floor. A neat, rather stout woman with gray hair arranged in a bun was seated on a couch.

Blount inclined his head. "I'm Inspector Blount, Mrs. Palmer."

"Yes, I heard."

"I've come to discuss the—er, disappearance of your daughter, Diana Palmer."

"Of course. Have you any news?"

"None, I'm sorry to say."

"Please sit down, Mr. Blount."

"Yes, ma'am." Blount took a chair. Uncle Dave stood in the corner.

"Just a few questions," said Blount. "I'd like to know where your daughter was flying to."

"To Bangalla," said Mrs. Palmer, fiddling with a small handkerchief.

"I see. To explore? I understand she's an explorer, as well as a number of other things."

"No. She wasn't going exploring. She was going to visit a—a friend."

"What is the friend's name?"

Mrs. Palmer hesitated. Blount leaned forward. As he did so, he became aware of a figure standing in the doorway leading to the next room. He glanced up.

The man was tall and rugged, dressed in a trench coat belted at the waist He had on dark glasses and a hat that covered most of his forehead. He was deeply tanned, although it was hard to make out his features.

"She was flying to Bangalla to see me, Inspector Blount." Blount blinked. The man's poise was unquestionable. He spoke in a deep, unaccented voice. And it was obvious that he was telling the truth.

"But if she was flying to Bangalla to see you, why are you here?"

"It's a difficult question to answer. Inspector."

"Perhaps if you tried," Blount suggested, his voice hardening. He did not want to tangle with the stranger in the weird outfit, but he could not let him go without trying to determine who he was and how he fitted into this odd puzzle.

"I am an old friend of Miss Palmer," the Phantom began, smiling faintly.

"That doesn't tell me anything. I'm afraid we'll have to take you along for questioning."

The Phantom shook his head, almost dreamily. "Sorry, but it's impossible."

Blount stood, moving toward the man.

And he vanished.

One moment he was standing in the doorway, and the next he was not there. Blount moved quickly into the doorway, looking to the right and left of the adjoining room. He saw the window open.

Crossing to it, he glanced down.

The man had evidently jumped out the window and escaped. But the ground was fifteen feet below. He would have to be quite an athlete to make it without breaking an ankle.

A bizarre thing.

Blount returned to the living room and frowned. He could

see that Diana Palmer's uncle was trying to avoid his look, and Mrs. Palmer was sobbing into her handkerchief.

The doorbell rang.

In a moment Uncle Dave was back in the living room holding a note in his hand.

Blount reached for the paper. The words were block-lettered in a crude hand: IF YOU WANT DIANA BACK SEND ONE MAN WITH 250 THOUSAND DOLLAR BILLS TO NORTH RIVER BRIDGE MIDNIGHT TOMORROW. NO POLICE OR NO DIANA.

Below the words was a drawing of a hangman's noose.

CHAPTER 6

Police Commissioner James Nolan flicked the switch on his intercom. "Yes, Nellie?"

"An Inspector Blount in on the wire, Commissioner. He's with the Federal Aviation Agency."

"It's about that airliner skyjack. Put him on; please."

"Commissioner Nolan? Inspector Blount here. We met a year ago on that skyjacking to Cuba."

"I remember, Inspector. What can I do for you?"

"I'm out at the Palmer residence. You know Miss Palmer was not among the passengers picked up."

"We've got some men working on her background, Inspector. We're trying to tie her in with the skyjackers."

"I've got news for you. There's been a ransom note."

"How much?"

"Two hundred and fifty thousand dollars."

The Commissioner whistled. "What do you think? Is it authentic? Or just a cover to screen her involvement?"

"It looks like the real thing to me, but I can't make anything out of the note."

"Is Dave Palmer there?"

"Yes."

"Let me talk to him. He's an old friend."

"Right."

In a moment David Palmer was on the wire. "Hello, Jim."

"I hear you've got a ransom note."

"A quarter of a million dollars for my niece, Jim."

"We'll take care of it for you."

"Please. I don't want you to do anything about it. The wording of the note is quite specific. It says that Diana will be killed if there is any police interference."

"Do you believe that? They always say that, Dave."

"I believe this note."

"We're old friends, Dave. You know I wouldn't do anything to hurt Diana. Now let me come out and personally talk this over with you."

"I'd rather not, Jim."

The Commissioner shook his head. "Please Dave. I promise not to do anything until I get an agreement from you. How's that?"

There was a pause. "All right, Jim."

"I'll be right over," said the Commissioner. "You just sit tight and wait."

"I won't be going anywhere."

Commissioner Nolan was a handsome man of forty-five who looked thirty-five. He was very athletic, slim and dapper. He was also independently wealthy, but had always worked in the civic interest. He had a personable way about him, was the most intelligent man in local politics, and knew all the important people in the area.

"Hi, Dave," he said as he came into the Palmer house. "Where's your lovely sister-in-law?"

Mrs. Palmer rose, smiling. "Hello, Jim."

"Well, Dorothy, it's a long time. You shouldn't be such a stranger."

"What would I want with the Police Commissioner?"

Nolan sank into the couch. "Inspector Blount tells me you've got a note."

"Yes." Dorothy turned to Dave. "Give it to Jim, please." Dave pulled a rumpled sheet of paper out of his suit coat pocket and handed it to Nolan. Then he took out his pipe and began sucking on it, watching Nolan closely.

Nolan studied the note carefully and then shook his head.

"Well, I don't understand the implications. The location of the ransom drop is obviously the North River Bridge on Main Street. But I don't understand the signature."

"Neither do I."

Nolan frowned. "Not that it would make any difference if I did. Still, I'd advise you to let us take this whole thing off your hands, Dave. It could get messy."

Uncle Dave shook his head. "Absolutely not, Jim. I said it on the phone, and I mean it. If we let you stick your nose into this, Diana will die."

"Not necessarily. We know about these things. We're

experienced in tracking down kidnappers. You must realize that a kidnapper does not kill because the cops are after him. He usually kills before he even delivers the ransom note."

Mrs. Palmer gasped. "Are you saying Diana might be dead already?"

Nolan bit his lip. "I suppose it did come out that way. I don't really think so. Not with the strange circumstances of Diana's kidnapping. It almost seems as if the skyjacker recognized Diana on the plane manifest and decided to kidnap her as an added bonus to the theft of the plane."

Uncle Dave leaned back. "What would you do if I gave you permission to go ahead and take care of the case, Commissioner?"

"I would have my experts work things out, Dave."

"I'll make a deal with you. I want an expert of my own to work on the case for twenty-four hours. Then you can have it."

"Those twenty-four hours may be crucial!"

"I realize that. Still, I'd like to let my own man take a shot at it."

Nolan leaned back. "Who is this expert, Dave? Somebody I know?"

"I sincerely doubt it."

Nolan rose and sighed. "If you insist, then. We're too good friends to argue. But the minute the twenty-four hours are up, it's our case."

"Right."

"'Bye, Dorothy," said Nolan as he walked out

It was dark when Dave Palmer left the house. He knew that the Phantom had merely left the Palmer mansion in order to avoid speaking to Inspector Blount about the skyjacking. Palmer had an idea that the Phantom knew all about the kidnapping. He had ways of finding out things in spite of every precaution taken to keep him unaware.

The Palmer estate stretched into the woods for a half mile. Palmer walked along the pathways, whistling softly and puffing on his pipe. He had lit it now, so that the smoke trailed behind him, leaving a pleasing aroma in the air.

He knew that the best way to find the Phantom was to let the Phantom find him.

Near a small waterfall in the stream that cut across the estate the Phantom came out of the shadows and hailed Dave.

"Well, that was quite a show you put on at the house," Palmer laughed.

"I had to think. I didn't want all those inspectors and bureaucrats around."

They sat down on a large boulder.

"There's been a kidnap note, Kit," said Palmer, removing the wrinkled sheet from his pocket.

The Phantom nodded. "I was close by and could hear a

great deal of what went on." He smiled. "I think I know what the signature means, but I'd like to study it a bit more." Palmer puffed on his pipe and waited.

Finally the Phantom glanced up. "It's a very serious situation," he said slowly. "It's a drawing of the Silken Noose."

"And what's the Silken Noose?"

"The symbol of an ancient secret fraternity. The Assassins."

"Assassins? I didn't know that was a secret fraternity! I thought an assassin was someone who killed a president or a ruler for some political reason."

"The word has come to mean that," the Phantom explained slowly. "Actually the word 'assassin' is from the Arabic 'hashshahin,' meaning the addict of the drug hashish, or Indian hemp, which is cousin to our own marijuana."

"But how did this secret fraternity start?"

"It was an order of religious fanatics, originating in the Ismaili branch of the Shiite sect. A Persian named al-Hasan iba-al-Sabbah, a Fatimid missionary, founded the sect in Iran during the twelfth century."

"Was it a religious movement of any consequence?"

"It had very little religious consequence at all. It was one of propaganda with little regard for spiritual objectives. At its head was the Shaykl-al-Jabal, known to the Crusaders in popular translation as 'The Old Man of the Mountain.' He was the chief of operations, and he was aided by two groups of subordinates, the Grand Priors, and below them, contingents of desperados ready to do or die in blind obedience to the command of their chief."

Palmer whistled. "It sounds monstrous. Whom did they kill?"

"Anyone in power," the Phantom explained. "Anyone opposed to their particular line of politics. In two hundred years, the Assassins spread their militant anarchical influence through many parts of the Moslem world by establishing a chain of hill forts in northern Iran and Syria and by pursuing a relentless policy of secret assassination against their enemies.

"One of their first victims was Hasan's old schoolmate, Nizam-al-Mulk, patron of learning and vizier of the sultan, Malik Shah, who had sent out two unsuccessful expeditions against the order."

"How have they managed to last this long?"

"They haven't, really. But while they lasted they were very strong. Toward the close of the twelfth century the Assassins gained a foothold in northern Syria, where the hill fortress of Masyad served them as an impregnable citadel. Their chief in Syria, Rash'd-al-Din Sinan, one of the Old Men of the Mountain, terrorized the invading Crusaders in a campaign of systematic murder.

"Then in 1265 the Persian strongholds of the order were destroyed by the Mongols under Hulagu. In 1272 those in Syria were demolished by the Mameluke ruler, Baybars I, and the Assassins of Syria were scattered. Remnants of the sect exist today in northern Syria, Iran, Zanzibar, Oman, and India. But generally speaking, the Assassins were wiped out in 1300 or so."

"But who are these members?"

The Phantom shook his head. "I have no idea. But if that silken noose is any proof, we're in big trouble."

"What should we do?"

"I want to deliver that ransom money to the kidnappers," the Phantom said.

"You? But I don't know where I can get a quarter of a million dollars that quickly."

"Don't worry about it."

"But where's the money?"

The Phantom flexed his biceps and grinned at Uncle Dave. "Right here in this strong right arm."

Palmer turned pale. "You—you're going to—to bluff them?"

"No. I'm going to catch them."

CHAPTER 7

The fog rolled in from the sea at eleven o'clock, and by midnight it was difficult to see five paces in front of one's nose. On the river, the mists rose thickly, coiling about the railings and the spans of the bridge which crossed wide North River in the center of town.

A steady burbling sound rose from the water below the bridge. As the Phantom, in trench coat and hat, slipped out of the darkness and came to the walkway that crossed the bridge, he paused a moment to listen. He heard the muffled roar of a powerboat engine on the river. No cars were about.

Peering through the mist, the Phantom's sharp eyes made out the silhouette of a figure standing in the middle of the bridge.

"He's waiting for the ransom money," the Phantom mused. "He's been ordered to take the money, lower it to the boat, and possibly jump down himself. That's the scheme."

The Phantom backed into the shadows formed by one of the transverse steel beams supporting the bridge. If he was not mistaken, he had heard another sound as he stood there, a scuffing that was not quite obscured by the noise of the boat's engine. Footsteps, behind him?

"It's either one of the kidnappers, waiting to close in on me, or it's a police tail," the Phantom thought. "The problem becomes academic. I must show myself. Then the police will know enough not to attack me. Together we can take the man on the bridge. If the second man is not a police tail, he must be one of the Assassins. In which case I'll have to lure them both onto the bridge and fight them there."

The Phantom waited another several minutes, but the footsteps behind him had ceased.

He stepped out into the shrouded light of a street lamp that burned at the edge of the bridge, illuminating the walkway along the span. At that moment he turned to look behind him, allowing anyone following him a chance to see him.

Then he started walking to the center of the bridge. As he did so, he deliberately removed his fedora and dark glasses, and he turned once again so that his pursuer would know exactly who he was.

Quickly he donned his hat and glasses and started moving toward the shrouded figure in the middle of the bridge.

He could hear running feet behind him and a shout in the night. The shout was uttered in a foreign tongue which the Phantom did not recognize, although he was master of eighteen languages and partially fluent in twenty-six others.

Whatever the running man behind him had said, it spurred the man on the bridge into action. Before the Phantom reached him, the waiting Assassin climbed to the railing and jumped into the river. As the Phantom turned to face the man behind him, he could see that he too had climbed to the railing and jumped into the misty waters below.

He smiled to himself and immediately vaulted onto the railing. Without a seconds hesitation, he leaped out into the air, diving headfirst into the water, executing a perfect swan dive from the edge of the high bridge. He cleaved the water expertly, scarcely raising a ripple as he did so. He rose to the surface almost instantly, shaking his head and flicking the water out of his eyes.

He could see the powerboat, now with exhaust burbling out of the water in a noxious cloud at its aft end. Between him and the boat were two heads bobbing in the water, floundering toward the hull.

Now the Phantom could hear voices, this time speaking in broken English.

"Where is the ransom money, you fool?" asked one voice. The Phantom could see the speaker leaning over the side of the powerboat and reaching out to assist one of the swimmers.

"There's no money."

"No money? Then why did you jump?"

"Phantom! Phantom!"

"What's all this about a ghost?"

"No! Ghost Who Walks! He came in the night. I could see his face."

"Fool! No one sees the Phantom's face."

"The mask. The hood. I saw the Phantom!"

"If you're lying. Kali will kill you."

"I never lie. Get me aboard."

There was the sound of splashing and cursing.

"Help me up!" another voice called.

The Phantom moved slowly toward the powerboat, circling it to approach from the opposite side. He could see three men on board, peering out into the gloom.

"I heard a splash. He's dived in after us!"

"Are you sure?"

"Positive. Look, isn't that him?"

"I can't see—but, yes!"

"I'll shoot him."

"Hold it," snapped the first voice. "Kali said there was to be no shooting. Sound attracts police. Come on. We've got to use our heads."

"What shall we do?"

"We'll cut him to ribbons with the propellers of the boat."

The Phantom could hear the sound of the boat engine revving up. He treaded water, realizing he could not get to the side of the craft before it began moving. The propellers were a distinct threat to him. If the Assassins on the boat could locate him, they would certainly run right over him.

As he thought of this, and tried to plan a counteraction, a bright yellow spotlight blazed in the fog, casting its light in the Phantom's eyes.

"There he is!" a voice shouted triumphantly.

The powerboat engine gunned up, and the Phantom could hear it cutting through the water toward him.

The Phantom had always been a good swimmer. From his days as a youth in the jungle of Bangalla, he had swum for hours at a time and had practiced underwater diving along with the pygmies of the jungle. He had been known throughout the area for his speed, endurance, and ability to stay underwater for long periods of time.

Now he gulped in a breath of air and plunged down into the waters of North River, opening his eves underwater to try to make out the powerboat coming toward him on the water's surface. The three Assassins had left the spotlight turned on, which enabled him to see the form of the boat's hull as it approached.

Quickly he squirmed out of his trench coat, which he wore

over his Phantom suit, and bundled it into a wad in his hands. Then he shot upward, finning toward the craft above him with his powerful legs, timing his shot. He reached the propellers at thg stem of the boat just as it passed over him, and thrust the trench coat into the blades.

There was a grinding sound and a great flurry of foam in the water all around him.

The Phantom swam away, remaining underwater as long as he could. The powerboat was several yards from him when he surfaced. The spotlight had been turned in toward the edge of the hull.

Treading water silently, the Phantom watched the three figures on board. He could hear their voices as they spoke to one another, but he could not distinguish which one was speaking.

"I tell you, I heard those propellers hit something."

"But can you be sure it was the Ghost Who Walks?"

"What else?"

"Let's go back," said a third voice. "I'll circle around and maybe we can find proof of his death."

"Yes. I would not want to report to Kali our failure and not be able to swear the Ghost Who Walks is now dead." The Phantom decided that the speaker was the leader of the group and had been the one left aboard the powerboat.

The craft circled slowly around, the spotlight probing through the mist.

"Hold up! There! You see it?"

"Yes! It's something floating."

"Get that grappling pole."

"Here. Look. It's a piece of clothing."

"That's it! The Phantom's coat! That's the coat he was wearing over his suit!"

"Are you sure?"

"Yes!"

"I saw it too. It's the Ghost Who Walks, all right."

"Then the propellers did their work. He's dead. The Ghost Who Walks is no more!"

There was excited laughter.

The Phantom swam quickly toward the craft. "Playful bunch of Assassins," he mused. "And to think Diana's in their hands."

He could hear the voices continue as he swam.

"I hate to report to Kali that two sworn Assassins have run like frightened sheep at the sight of a mere man."

"But it was the Ghost Who Walks!"

"We swear it!"

"Yet he is now dead, killed like any normal man, by the propellers of our powerboat."

"Then we are lucky. It was the Phantom."

"Very well. We'll report it that way. I think you're both chicken-hearted cowards."

"You'd have run too, if you'd seen him."

"Not me," snarled the voice of the man who the Phantom knew was their leader.

With his silent crawl, the Phantom was approaching the hull of the boat. He could see a mooring line hanging down the side of the craft near the stem. He grasped it quietly and again took a breath and lowered himself into the water where he could not be seen.

"I'll take one more look out there," said one of the Assassins.

The spotlight revolved all the way around the boat, shining through the mist and lighting up the quickly flowing current of the river.

"Okay. He's not there. He's sunk to the bottom, I'm sure."

"Let's go. We've got to report that we didn't get the ransom to Kali."

"We must be sure to point out that we have destroyed the Phantom."

The engine began throbbing in a higher tone, and the craft moved downstream toward the sea.

Holding onto the line, the Phantom came up for air, twisting the line around his hands to prevent it from slipping out of his grasp.

"I've got to hang onto this murderous trio and let them lead me to Diana," he said to himself.

Where was Diana? he wondered. Obviously many miles from here. Unless the kidnappers had circled back and brought the skyjacked airliner to the United States.

Highly unlikely.

The Assassins had spoken of reporting to Kali. Did that mean they were in radio contact with him? Or that he was physically present at the rendezvous toward which they were now headed?

The Phantom hoped it was the latter.

CHAPTER 8

When Diana Palmer first awoke, she could not for the life of her remember where she was. Then, as she studied the interior of the airliner and looked through the porthole at the dawning day outside, the memory of the night before flooded back into her consciousness.

She sat up straight, to find that she had gone to sleep in one of the seats in a reclining position. The aircraft was no longer in flight, but was bobbing up and down on water. She clambered over to the seat next to her and peered outside.

The plane had landed in a kind of lagoon, with a sparkling white beach beyond and numerous palm trees and thick vines bordering it. The beach was deserted. The terrain rose slightly to a sloping hill, topped with volcanic minerals and some small tropical trees.

The plane was moored to a wharf built out into the sparkling blue water. Beyond the wharf she could see more beach, and on top of a rocky hill a large structure was built in the shape of an ancient castle. It reminded her of pictures in books she had read at school showing castles the Crusaders had built in the Middle Ages.

She stood immediately and began to walk down the aisle to the back door of the plane. At the same moment, the door to the cockpit opened, and Kali stepped through. He saw her instantly, and smiled. He was not wearing his hat, but was smoking his ubiquitous cigarette. He seemed untired although she knew he had slept even less than she had.

"I thought I heard a stirring out here. Did you have a nice rest, Miss Palmer?"

"As nice as could reasonably be expected," she snapped. "Where are we?"

"We are at our destination, as you can see."

"Where is that?"

Kali smiled. "That would be telling, Miss Palmer. Suffice it to say it is an island and not a continent. I mention this merely to warn you in advance that it is quite impossible for you to escape from it."

"An island? In the Caribbean?"

"Not every ocean is contiguous to the American land mass, Miss Palmer," said Kali softly. "Perhaps yes. Perhaps no. Let us leave it at that."

"I promise you that I will try to escape if you continue to try to hold me."

"I shall hold you, Miss Palmer, until the ransom is paid for your release," Kali spoke severely. "There is no escape from this island. I own it. I also own access to and egress from it." Diana bit her lip. It was obvious that Kali was not lying.

"Do you have a summer home here?"

Kali laughed. "I have all my followers here, Miss Palmer."

"Followers? Are you a—a god of some kind?" Diana couldn't conceal her sarcasm.

"Indeed not. There is but one Supreme Being, Miss Palmer." Kali glowered at her sternly. "However, I am the leader of a large group of people who believe as I do. Let us leave it at that."

"What kind of group?"

"A religious sect."

"I don't believe it. You're just a cheap crook who's decided to skyjack a plane and collect ransom for a kidnapping."

Kali smiled faintly. "Perhaps that is the way it seems to you, Miss Palmer, but I assure you, there is a great deal more to it than that."

"Oh? What?"

Kali shook his head. "I have no time to talk." He took her arm. "Come. Let us go ashore. I, for one, am very hungry, and I am sure you must be famished yourself."

Diana frowned. "Where are the two men who helped you skyjack the plane?"

"I have dismissed them. I presume they are in their own quarters ashore."

"And the seamen from the boat?"

"They too have gone ashore to their families."

"Then the island is inhabited."

"By my followers," Kali said.

"If your group is so large, I don't see why you have to stoop to such underhanded methods of achieving your ends."

"There is always the problem of financial backing," Kali observed, puffing elegantly on his cigarette. "My actions are simply in response to that rather pressing demand."

Diana fumed, but said nothing.

"Come, let us go eat."

There was a gangplank leading from the entrance of the plane to the wharf. Kali led Diana down it, and Diana felt the solid planking of the wharf under her feet. It was the first time she had felt the security of the earth since leaving her mother and uncle so long ago at home.

She felt a sudden pang. How were they taking this thing? Their steps clattered on the wharf as they crossed it to the sand, and Kali pointed out the hills and the beaches on either side of the wharf.

"That's my home," said Kali a moment later, gesturing toward the castle on the rock.

"It's more like a palace," snorted Diana, trying to get a rise out of her host, but failing.

"In point of fact, it is a castle. The Moors originally constructed it, but it was rebuilt by the Crusaders when they came through this way in the thirteenth century."

"Just who are you?" she asked suddenly.

Kali laughed. "Henry Kali, in your tongue, my dear."

"And in yours?"

"Sheik-al-Jabal."

"You're Arabic?" Diana asked quickly.

"Not at all. Those of my sect subscribe to Moorish customs, in part, but we are not a segment of the Muslim faith. We take Arabic names from history. It is simply a way of identifying ourselves."

"And you come from what country originally?"

"That is for me to know and no one else," Kali intoned.

They walked along a path that rose from the beach. It was hewn from the rocky outcrop overhanging the ocean. Waves crashed on the rocks below, throwing spume high into the air.

Diana paused a moment to look off across the water. It was a beautiful sight—pure blue water all the way to the horizon and blue sky above. There wasn't anything in sight, except seagulls wheeling and squawking above them. Except for the sound of the birds, there was an almost pristine silence overhanging the scene.

"Lovely," said Diana.

"Of course." Kali waved his cigarette in the air.

They continued on up the pathway until it led them into a courtyard surrounded by large ironwood trees. Tables and chairs had been set out under the trees.

"We occasionally dine out here," said Kali, indicating the furniture. "It's very peaceful."

Kali took her across the courtyard to a walk leading around the side of the castle wall. Diana could see seagulls flying around the buttresses of the tower.

The walk passed another open yard which had a stone wall at least eight feet high built around it. Diana felt her heart leap into her throat. She drew back, gripping Kali's arm compulsively.

"No!"

Kali smiled. "He's quite harmless, even if I say so."

Diana was staring in fright at an enormous gorilla linked to the rock wall by a heavy chain attached to an iron collar around his neck. The beast was staring at Diana with hatred in his eyes, but he did not move.

"You see, he never moves when I am around." Kali laughed.

"Why do you have such a beast?"

"To keep some people out." Kali chuckled. "And to keep others in."

"To kill your prisoners if they try to escape?" Diana asked lightly, trying to smile.

"Exactly. One doesn't need to be subtle with you, does one, Miss Palmer?" He removed Diana's hand from his arm. Diana was embarrassed and moved away from Kali. "His name is Toto," Kali told her after a moment.

At the sound of his name, the big gorilla rose to his-feet, pulled at his ponderous chain, and pounded his fists at his breast, uttering a strange lonely bellow.

"Yes," said Kali. "You see? He's glad to see me. Aren't you, Toto, old boy?"

Diana cringed. "See you? I think he wants to eat you."

"Perhaps," said Kali. "Well, he will never get the chance."

They moved away from Toto, who watched them go with glowering intensity. Diana looked back once and shuddered. The gorilla was eyeing her with disdain, shaking his chains and growling deep in his throat.

Kali led Diana into the castle through an outside door, and soon they were walking along a dimly lit interior corridor. Steps led down from the corridor, and Kali took Diana's hand and helped her go down them. They were old-fashioned stone steps that must have been cut for the original structure. Diana was intrigued by the ancient architecture and kept looking up at the niches cut in the wall for the placement of oil lamps and candles.

There was a smell of dampness and fetid age in the air. Diana shuddered, her fascination with the architecture evaporating instantly. They came out into a narrow corridor, and there, in front of them, stood a door with iron bars on it.

"In here," said Kali.

Diana drew back, her arms raised in defense. "Please! Not in there!"

"It's quite clean." Kali gripped her mercilessly and pulled her along with him. "I can always call my men to help, you know."

Diana let herself be led through the door into a room which was actually quite pleasant even though it had almost no furniture and only one large barred window cut high in the stone wall.

"I have to stay here?"

"Only until your ransom is paid, Miss Palmer."

Diana sat down on the rather comfortable chair, which, along with the bed, were the only articles of furniture in the cell.

"And what if they don't pay?" Diana wondered, thinking of the difficulty her mother and uncle might have in raising all that money in cash.

Kali removed the dead cigarette butt from his holder and stamped it out on the floor.

"Then, my dear, you will be destroyed. And so will they. All must be destroyed. We don't want any loose ends around."

"Not Mom and Uncle Dave, too!"

"Certainly. We are a very tidy sect. We do things up neatly. No loose ends." He chuckled.

CHAPTER 9

When the powerboat manned by the three Assassins finally pulled in toward a small jetty in the ghetto section of the city, the Phantom quietly let go of the line, submerged, and swam underwater until he was under the protection of the small ramshackle dock.

With the engine turned off, the leader of the three leaped onto the jetty and made a line fast to a stanchion.

The other two clambered to the dock after him.

"We have to report in at once," said the leader, whose voice the Phantom was beginning to recognize.

"Kali will be furious."

"It wasn't our fault. We did our best."

"Come on. Let's stop all this foolish talk and get back to the radio room."

The Phantom heard the sound of their steps moving away from the jetty. He pulled himself up onto the jetty and crouched there, watching the three figures as they walked off past the docking area which was littered with broken bottles and tin cans. Beyond it there was an alleyway bordered by wooden fences.

The Phantom slipped along in the darkness after them, keeping in the shadows and making no sound.

The man in the lead, who had a shining bald head, was the

tallest of the three. He was easily distinguishable from the others. The other two were of similar size, about six feet, one with an old-fashioned butch crewcut, and the other with long curly hair. They all wore tee shirts and slacks for ease in movement.

One of the three—the one with the crewcut—suddenly halted and turned around, peering into the darkness near where the Phantom had frozen into immobility, "I got the funniest idea we're being followed."

"Nonsense," growled the bald man. "It's just your imagination."

The one with the curly hair shook his head. "I have the same feeling."

For a moment, Baldy contemplated the shadows behind him. Then he waved his arm impatiently.

"Let's go. You're just imagining things. No one follows us. We—the Assassins—follow others."

Crewcut turned docilely and walked after Baldy. After a moment, Curly brought up the rear, still glancing back over his shoulder as the three of them continued down the alleyway.

The Phantom waited until they had turned the corner before he made his next move. He sped up to the end of the fence and peered around it. He was just in time. The three of them were turning in through a gateway. Behind a wooden wall there was a large warehouse.

Waiting until the door had creaked open and the three had vanished into the darkness of the building, the Phantom hurried after them. He stood against the door and pressed his ear to it. He could hear the sound of footsteps. When he could not distinguish the sound any longer, he tugged at the handle.

The door opened.

He found himself in a high-ceilinged structure. The floor was covered with crates and boxes at one end, and smaller bundles of cardboard boxes and piles of junk at the other. A way had been cleared through one side, and at the end of the passageway a door stood open. Beyond that there was a glow of light.

Quickly the Phantom made his way along the cleared sector of the warehouse and came to the open door. Stairs led down from the door into a cellar or basement of some kind. It was from that area that he could hear the muffled sound of voices.

The Phantom had always been blessed with perfect hearing—hearing a great deal more acute than the average person's. He closed his eyes now to concentrate on the sounds from the room below the warehouse.

"Flip on that switch, will you?" Crewcut was saying.

"It's on." That was Curly.

"It'll take a minute to warm up. You better write out what to say."

"I'm doing that now, idiot," Baldy said.

"How can we explain the Phantom?" Curly wondered.

"Let me handle that," Baldy said. "The important thing is that we failed to get the ransom."

"In a few seconds we'll be ready to transmit," Crewcut announced.

There was a short silence.

"Give me that note," said Crewcut.

The Phantom could hear the rustle of paper.

"4XC3," said Curly. "4XC3. Come in, 4XC3."

"Any answer?" Baldy asked.

"Not yet. 4XC3, calling 4XC3—"

Suddenly there was a scratchy sound of static and a faint electronic Voice responded distantly:

"4XC3 here. Can you hear me, 7FG3?"

"Yes. We have contact."

"What is your message, 7FG3? Mention no names. Just tell me if the mission was a success."

The Phantom moved swiftly, leaping down the steps soundlessly, drawing the Colt .45 out of his waterproof holster as he did so. A small room opened off to the left side of the steps. Behind a wooden railing the Phantom crouched. He could see the occupants of the room very clearly under the bright bulb hanging from the ceiling of the room.

A large radio transmitter-receiver stood against one of the cement-block walls of the room. A small table had been placed near it. At the table sat Crewcut, holding a microphone in his hand.

To one side of him stood Curly, watching.

Baldy, his head gleaming like a billiard ball in the light, was leaning on the table, close to Crewcut, prompting him by pointing to the slip of paper unfolded on the table top.

"Yes, 4XC3," said Crewcut. "The mission was—"

The Phantom aimed the handgun at the microphone and fired just as Crewcut spoke the last three words. The sound of the explosion echoed loudly in the small room. Simultaneously the microphone exploded in Crewcut's hand.

The Phantom moved then, jumping to the bottom of the steps, and advancing to cover all three men with the weapon in his hand.

Baldy was the first to recover from the shock. He swung around and saw the Phantom there. His eyes widened.

Curly was slower. He fell back against the transmitter in surprise when he saw the Phantom. His mouth dropped open. "You!"

Crewcut was stunned and did not turn. He simply stared at the shattered remnant of the microphone in his hand.

"The Ghost Who Walks!" croaked Baldy.

"But—but you're—dead—" stammered Curly.

Crewcut finally turned around. When he saw the Phantom, he turned white and dropped the microphone holder as if it were on fire.

"The Phantom!"

"Sit very still," the Phantom ordered calmly. "The three of you are coming with me. The police will be as anxious to question you as I am. We'd like particularly to know exactly where you were making your radio call to. That will be where Diana Palmer is."

Baldy smiled faintly. "We're sworn to silence. You won't get anything out of us."

"Won't we?" the Phantom commented pleasantly. "I think we will. You haven't a chance, you know. There's no way for you to escape. And I doubt your mentor Kali will be coming to rescue you."

"Possibly not Kali," Crewcut said boldly, "but someone else will."

"Our group is large and powerful," said Baldy smugly.

"I know all about your sect of Assassins." The Phantom straightened resolutely. "We'll break it up, and you won't have a prayer."

"You're only one man," said Baldy. "How do you plan to take the three of us with you now?" His eyes were beginning to narrow.

"If you don't believe I can do it, just try something."

Crewcut rose from the table where he had been sitting and faced the Phantom. "I'll go along quietly. I've heard about you."

The Phantom smiled.

Baldy turned red with anger. "What is this? Mutiny?" He stepped toward Crewcut menacingly.

At that moment Curly was completely out of the line of fire, screened by his two companions. That was the moment he chose to throw a long thin cord at the Phantom's gun hand. The end of the cord was fastened to a heavy lead weight.

The lead weight slid past the Phantom's wrist, dropped, and swung back. Then, drawn tightly on the cord, it circled the Phantom's wrist for three turns. Quickly Curly jerked hard on the Phantom's wrist, jarring the weapon from his hand.

Too late the Phantom realized what had happened. The weighted cord was an ancient weapon which had been used in Biblical times to kill and retrieve game all in one motion.

Baldy projected himself toward the Phantom with Crewcut right after him. Too late, the Phantom thought, crouching and pulling aside, trying at the same time to retrieve his Colt which lay on the concrete floor.

But Curly pulled hard again and threw the Phantom off balance with the cord and weight still attached to his wrist. The Phantom was forced to twist frantically at the weight and cord which was cutting into his flesh most painfully.

Crewcut slashed at the Phantom's neck with karate chops and Baldy pummeled him with blows to the chest and stomach. The Phantom was on the concrete floor then, with his two assailants on top of him.

Finally he succeeded in loosening the cord and weight. At that moment, Curly tugged hard on the empty cord, going over backwards and howling as his head hit the edge of the table.

Baldy smashed the Phantom's jaw with his fist, and the Phantom fell back himself. A heavy weight plunged into him, and then he felt a blow in the solar plexus that forced all the breath out of his body.

He slumped there.

When he was able to rise, he saw with blurred vision that the room was deserted.

The light was still on.

Staggering and rubbing his sore body, he clutched the back of the chair in which Crewcut had been seated while he sent his radio message to Kali.

The Phantom's vision began clearing.

He saw the scribbled note on the table in front of him. And then, to one side, he saw another piece of paper.

On it was written two words: TYDORE NEXT.

CHAPTER 10

In the office of Police Commissioner James Dolan, the Phantom sat quietly waiting for Dolan to finish reading the report on the incidents following his attempt to catch the kidnappers of Diana Palmer.

Adjusting his dark glasses and tightening the belt of his trench coat, the Phantom leaned forward and said, "I typed it myself to save you the trouble, Commissioner. I also wanted it to be accurate."

Dolan nodded and glanced up. "Well, this seems very detailed and accurate." He cleared his throat. "My men are going over that warehouse and basement radio station with a fine-toothed comb. As yet we haven't discovered much of anything. The warehouse is owned by a group of businessmen who rented it out to a firm of importers. The importers subleased the basement to a third group, but there's no record of them."

"What about the radio transmitter? Couldn't they make contact with Kali by simply using the same call letters?"

"We tried that." Dolan stood up and paced back and forth. "One of the Assassins had taken the precaution of resetting the wavelength, and so even if we had made the call, no one there would have responded."

The Phantom shook his head glumly. "It was stupidity on

my part to be taken like that. Overconfidence. It won't happen again."

"Let's not worry about it. Walker. After all, you did bring us this note about Tydore."

"That's what I wanted to check on." The Phantom looked up eagerly. "Does that name ring any bell?"

"As a matter of fact, it does." Dolan seated himself again and began swinging back and forth in his swivel chair.

"Tydore is the ruler of a small principality called Tydia. It was a French protectorate many years ago, but is now an independent little constitutional monarchy. Tydore is the king at present. His son is the prince—a man about forty-five. There is a royal line of Tydores. The present king is probably the twelfth or thirteenth."

"But how does Tydore tie in with Kali's piracies?"

Dolan steepled his fingers and leaned toward the Phantom. 'The point is, Prince Tydore is in the city now after two visits to Washington."

"Here?" The Phantom sat up.

"That's right."

" 'Tydore next,' " the Phantom repeated under his breath. "Do you think that means that the trio of Assassins is going to strike again right here in the city?"

"Why not?" Dolan responded. "With the ransom for Diana Palmer in the works, they could just as easily strike again."

"You feel they are going to kidnap the prince?"

"Possibly. However, there's an even better chance they might go after the Prince's daughter, Naji."

"A princess?"

"Right."

"How do you plan to guard the Prince and his daughter?"

Dolan looked away. "Actually we can't, Walker. We're under strict budgetary surveillance at the moment. I simply can't turn out two hundred and fifty patrolmen to keep watch on that parade."

The Phantom blinked. "There is to be a parade?"

"This afternoon at two o'clock. They're going from City Hall to the Hotel Majestic. It's all very regal, and good public relations."

"And you can't post sharpshooters on the buildings to watch out for any funny business?"

"I told you. I'm on a tight budget. We'll do all we can, of course, but I simply can't part with any more men."

"Can you get the Prince to call off the parade?"

The Commissioner sighed. "We've tried that, of course. But it simply won't work. This is his big moment."

The Phantom stood up and walked over to the window to

look out. "Maybe I'd better try to help you."

"I think you've done enough, Walker," the Commissioner said. "After all, taking on those three Assassins by yourself like that—you could have gotten hurt."

"Only my pride," said the Phantom ruefully.

Dolan chuckled. "I wish I could say we were able to call off the parade, but I'm afraid we can't."

"Thanks, Commissioner. I appreciate your help."

"Sorry I don't have any good news about Diana Palmer."

The Phantom nodded grimly.

The five cars moved slowly as they made their way along the street toward the hotel where Prince Tydore and his daughter Naji were staying. In his belted trench coat, dark glasses, and hat, the Phantom stood inconspicuously alongside the street, watching the lead car drive by.

It was a convertible limousine with the top down. The two figures in the back seat beamed out at the crowd and waved their hands gaily.

The Phantom could see them clearly. The Prince was a middle-aged man with a rather round face, thinning black hair, and a pug nose that gave his face a look of continual bewilderment. He was dressed in Western clothes which seemed to be rather uncomfortable for him.

At his side sat a beautiful young woman in her early twenties. She had long brown hair, gray eyes, and a slender, well-formed body. She was wearing a simple dress, cut low in front. She was laughing gaily,

The crowds sent up a big cheer as the cortège came along. The mayor was in one car, the president of the city council in another, and a raft of politicians in a third. The parade continued past the Phantom toward the center of the city.

It turned away from the main street and went down a side street. The Phantom kept pace with it on foot. He did not have to walk very fast. The traffic signals caught the cars at every corner.

Suddenly the Phantom moved over to the edge of the sidewalk against a building and peered ahead of him in the crowd. It was Crewcut! He recognized him, even though he was now wearing a pair of slacks, a shirt open at the collar, and a sports jacket over that. A telltale bulge in Crewcut's jacket attracted the Phantom's eye: it was a gun.

The Phantom was torn between pursuing Crewcut immediately to prevent him from taking action against the Prince's car and telephoning the Commissioner for help.

He knew it would take too long for help to arrive and opted

for the immediate pursuit of Crewcut. With that in mind, he forced his way through the crowd and tried to reach the Assassin.

Luck was against him. The signal changed at the very moment he started forward, and a crowd of humanity, released by the light, surged across the street and onto the sidewalk directly in front of the Phantom.

He was caught like a chip in a stream. Directly ahead of him, he could see the cortège of cars moving along slowly, but he could not push his way through to reach Crewcut, who was also following them.

"Watch it, buddy!" snapped a man as the Phantom pushed against him, trying to force his way ahead.

"Sorry, sorry," said the Phantom.

"Hey, he must think he's a movie actor," a fat woman said as the Phantom pushed past her.

The Phantom was usually very polite, and he never offended anyone if it was at all possible to avoid doing so. But he was in a hurry now, and in no mood to apologize.

He pushed forward.

His attention had been momentarily diverted from Crewcut. Suddenly he found himself face to face with the man!

Crewcut stared, his eyes widened, and he turned and broke through the crowd which had almost magically thinned, running back the way he had come.

"Stop that man!" shouted the Phantom.

"What's with him?" someone growled.

"Stop him! He's a killer!"

The crowd opened up.

Crewcut was running hard, heading for the open door of a shop. The Phantom began gaining on him.

The Assassin dashed in through the shop doors and ran pell mell down the aisle for the rear.

The Phantom was right behind him when a clerk stepped out from behind a cash register, directly in his path.

"Could I help you. sir?" he asked, staring in surprise at the Phantom's belted trench coat and heavy dark glasses.

"Sorry. I'm trying to locate a friend of mine," panted the Phantom.

"I assume he owes you money." The clerk raised an eyebrow and turned to survey the store. "Where is he?"

The Phantom looked over the clerk's shoulder. There was no one in the store.

"I—I swear I saw him come in."

"It's probably those dark glasses, mister," suggested the clerk.

The Phantom was studying the back of the store very carefully. There were two rest rooms: one labeled MEN and the other, WOMEN.

"Could I use your rest room a moment?" he asked politely.

The clerk shrugged.

The Phantom ran down the aisle and plunged in through the door to the men's room.

There was no one inside.

At the rear there was a window, pushed up high, wide open.

The Phantom ran over to it and peered out.

A narrow alleyway extended along the back of the store. There were packing crates and refuse cans out there, but no Crewcut.

Nevertheless the Phantom vaulted through the window and ran up the alleyway in the direction toward which the parade was heading.

It was when he reached the sidewalk that he heard the wild screams and the screeching brakes.

CHAPTER 11

Instantly the Phantom understood what had happened. While he had been neatly maneuvered into chasing Crewcut, Curly had suddenly leaped out of the crowd surrounding the parade on the sidewalk and grabbed the driver of Prince Tydore's car.

As the Phantom ran through the crowd, he could see the driver struggling valiantly with the long-haired Assassin. The crowd remained panic-stricken along the side of the street. No one seemed willing to try to protect the Prince and Princess by fighting off the vicious Assassin.

The Phantom found himself unable to make his way through the tightly packed people on the side of the street.

Then he was free and able to see the car once again. Curly had by now thrown the driver out of the car. The front door hung open and Curly was pummeling the man on the sidewalk. The crowd drew back as the driver sank to the pavement unconscious.

At that moment the Phantom heard another cry from the crowd. Now Baldy appeared, holding, a gun and brandishing it at the crowd. He leaped onto the car and jumped into the rear seat, where he held the gun on Prince Tydore. The sovereign's face turned pale and he almost fainted. The Princess, the Phantom noted, was watching Baldy in astonishment. She did not seem to be frightened at all. She simply did not know what to do.

In the distance ahead, the lead cars had come to a halt, and several policemen were beginning to make their way through the crowd to the Prince's car. But the Phantom could see that it was going to take them much too long to get to the scene of the action.

Behind the car several horns were blaring, but no one was doing anything.

The Phantom pushed his way through the remaining few people between him and the car and jumped into the rear seat. Baldy had his back to him, menacing the Prince with the gun. The Princess stared in surprise at the Phantom but said nothing.

"Excuse me, please," the Phantom said to her and gripped Baldy's shoulders tightly.

Baldy swung around, his eyes going wide. "You again!" he croaked, swinging the gun around.

The Phantom clipped his wrist with a stiff-handed karate chop, and the Assassin's face grimaced with sudden pain. Reacting swiftly, he seized the Phantom by the neck and began choking him.

With the expertise of years of combat, the Phantom slipped his two forearms in between the Assassin's wrists and cracked the perspiring Assassin on the chin with both fists. Baldy slumped backward, and the weapon he had been holding fell to the floor of the open car. The Phantom reached down for it and, at the same moment, was struck on the head by the big man's elbow. Off-balance, the Phantom chopped at Baldy's head and got one arm under his left elbow. Pushing hard, he threw the big man into the front seat of the car.

At that moment, it lurched forward, leaving burning rubber on the pavement. The Phantom reached again for the gun on the floor but could not find it. It had apparently slipped under the seat when the Phantom hit Baldy.

Curly was at the wheel of the car, bulling his way through the crowd of people. Screams and curses sounded from the tightly packed group around the car. The Phantom was pushed back against Princess Naji by the quick acceleration.

Baldy turned, his face bleeding, and rose to smash his fist at the Phantom. The Phantom parried the blow easily, ducked his head, and brought his own elbow up into the big man's throat. Baldy lost his balance and fell heavily against the door of the car. In the violence, the latch had become jarred loose and the door opened.

At that moment, the car was making a very sharp left turn, and the centrifugal force of the maneuver threw the Assassin out into the alleyway.

The Phantom could hear his scream as he rolled against the wall of a building.

Quickly the Phantom hurled himself at Curly, grabbing a

handful of his long hair and pulling hard. Curly yelled but arched his back to keep the Phantom from lifting him bodily from the seat. The Phantom brought his left arm around Curly's throat in a half-hammerlock and pulled hard, using the leverage of the car seat to tear the Assassin out from behind the wheel.

Curly gripped the steering wheel tightly, but with the Phantom's leverage on his body, he was unable to steer the car adequately. Trying to arch against the Phantom's attack, Curly's foot pressed down on the gas pedal, and the car zoomed ahead, veering crazily to the left.

The car smashed against the wall of a building, caromed off, and hurtled in the opposite direction, smashing against the building on the right. There was a screech of rubber, the scream of metal, and the breaking of glass.

Curly's grip let go, and the Phantom dragged him over into the rear of the car. Both of them were on top of Prince Tydore.

The gas pedal, freed of Curly's weight, immediately returned to its neutral position. The car slammed against another building and came to a halt.

The Phantom pressed his fingers into Curly's neck at a pressure point, and the Assassin went limp in his arms.

The Phantom lifted him out of the car and laid him carefully on the sidewalk. The crowd was surging down the alley- way toward them. The Phantom was disappointed to see that Baldy had managed to escape, using the screen of the crowd to get away. There was no sign of Crewcut.

For a moment, the Phantom debated pursuing Baldy, but he knew it would be hopeless.

He turned quickly and bowed to Prince Tydore and the Princess.

"Are you all right, Your Majesty?" he asked politely. The Phantom had mingled enough with royalty to know that it was always wise to treat royalty as royalty, even though his instincts were to treat a king like anyone else.

"Yes," muttered the frightened little man. "What happened—and who are you?"

"I am Kit Walker," said the Phantom.

"I must thank you, Mr. Walker," said Prince Tydore.

"Allow me to congratulate you on your resourcefulness," said Princess Naji, smiling at the Phantom. "When everyone else was petrified, you acted."

The Phantom smiled faintly. "I am only sorry two of the Assassins have escaped."

"Two?" Prince Tydore repeated. "I saw only one other."

The Phantom shrugged. He did not feel like explaining

Crewcut's feint, particularly inasmuch as it had prevented the Phantom from stopping the attempt on Prince Tydore's life even sooner.

The crowd was now pressing in around the wrecked car. In the distance a patrolman was pushing his way through the throng.

"Hey, what's going on here?" the patrolman asked, puffing up to the car.

"There's been an attempt on the Prince's life," said the Phantom calmly.

"Yeah? Who are you?"

Prince Tydore struggled to regain his composure. "This is Mr. Walker. He saved my life—and the Princess's too. Now I'd suggest you get this crowd out of here and try to clean up this mess."

The policeman stared glumly at the Prince and then turned to the Phantom.

"Okay, mister. Now how come you got yourself involved in this? What right had you to interfere?"

"I saw a man holding a gun on the Prince, and I disarmed him."

Princess Naji spoke up. "Here's the weapon, Officer," she said tartly. "This man was helping us. I'd suggest you call your commanding officer and try to take charge of the man he caught for you."

The policeman flushed. "Right, lady." He took the weapon and glanced at it. "Yeah. Thirty-eight Smith and Wesson. Okay, mister. You'll have to come with me to Headquarters. Meanwhile, I'll call for the wrecker to get this crate out of the alleyway."

"An excellent suggestion. Sergeant," said the Phantom, who could see that the officer was not a sergeant at all. He pointed to Curly, slumped against the building. "Perhaps you could also do something about putting this man in custody."

"Uh, yeah," said Officer Railes.

The Phantom bowed to Prince Tydore and the Princess. "Perhaps we shall meet again, Prince Tydore."

The Prince smiled, glancing at his daughter. "I think that would be nice. Do you, Naji?"

Princess Naji smiled slowly. "I'd love it, Father." Her eyes were staring into the Phantom's with undisguised interest.

He adjusted his dark glasses and cleared his throat. "Anything Your Majesty wishes."

Police Commissioner Nolan stared abashed at the Phantom.

"Mr. Walker, it disturbs me to admit to you that you were completely right, we were completely wrong."

The Phantom held up a hand in mute appeal. "Please don't

go on about it, Commissioner. It's enough that I've managed to keep the Prince from harm."

"And the Princess," said Nolan.

"My main concern is still the safety of Diana Palmer. Have you had any word? Has Dave Palmer?"

"Nothing," said Nolan. "We're interrogating that suspect now."

"Has he told you where Henry Kali is hiding?"

The Commissioner shook his head, baffled. "He's apparently been well trained. He's holding out. Claims that someone will come to rescue him. 'We're bigger than anything you can stop,' he keeps telling my men." The Commissioner shook his head. "A very stubborn man."

"Perhaps it's more than will power," the Phantom mused. "He could be simply under post-hypnotic suggestion, you know. You couldn't get a word out of him then, even if you used truth serum."

"We don't intend to go that far," said the Commissioner, scandalized. "That wouldn't look good at all, you know."

The Phantom sighed. "I know it."

"Is there anything else we can do?"

"Put Prince Tydore and the Princess under surveillance," said the Phantom instantly.

Nolan sighed. "I've already contacted the mayor. It's not feasible."

"Not feasible?"

"Politically very bad," muttered Nolan. "The public relations could be very damaging to him and his administration."

"But the two of them are still in danger! And there are at least two Assassins at large right now! They're going to strike again—you know that!"

"My hands are tied," sighed Nolan.

CHAPTER 12

Two men were alone in the small office with the blinds drawn. One of them, six feet tall, with a billiard-ball head, was peering through the slats of the blind with an intense expression. His companion was a crewcut brute of a man with heavily muscled shoulders and a grim face.

"It's a range of no more than a hundred yards," said Baldy, tinning from the window.

Crewcut nodded. He leaned down and opened a large suitcase standing on the floor beside the only desk in the room. He rose holding a Remington deer rifle in his hands. He smiled down at it lovingly.

"The customs inspector didn't even ask to open up the bags," he chuckled to Baldy.

Baldy drew away from the window. "Stop the chatter, and let's get that scope sight mounted."

Crewcut frowned and reached into the suitcase for it. Baldy watched him as he fastened it carefully to the barrel of the Remington and then lifted the rifle to his shoulder and sighted through it.

"Well?" Baldy was impatient,

"It's fine."

"Get out the tripods," snapped Baldy. "We haven't got all day."

Crewcut grumbled and reached into the suitcase again.

He brought out two sturdy metal tripods, twelve inches high with adjustable clamps attached to their tops. The clamps were large enough to fit around the stock of the deer rifle.

"Help me," said Crewcut, gesturing to the desk.

Baldy nodded. Together the two of them pushed the scarred desk over to the window. Baldy pushed a chair out of the way, and then he came around behind Crewcut while he placed the tripods on the desk top. Then he fastened one near the muzzle and the other just forward of the trigger guard.

"Ready?"

Crewcut nodded. He pulled up a second chair and sat down at the desk. The telescopic sight was directly in front of him. He peered through it

"Lift the slat."

Baldy had leaned over the desk and pulled two of the blind slats apart so Crewcut could look through the window at the building across the street.

"What floor?"

"Fifth," snapped Baldy.

"I'm on the sixth."

"Lower the damned thing."

Crewcut reached out and loosened the setting on the rear tripod and raised it slowly, peering through the telescopic sight as he did so. A window on the fifth floor came into view. He could see men inside the room across the way. The sight made it seem as if they were only yards away.

"I don't see him," he told Baldy.

"He'll be there. Our man has the interrogation schedule."

"Right."

Crewcut tightened the screws on the tripod and peered through the scope sight once again. He was looking right in through the window at the men inside. He carefully moved the barrel tripod to the left until the rifle was aimed at the opposite side of the desk where there was an empty chair.

"Got it?" Baldy asked impatiently.

"Got it."

Baldy let the slats fall into place. Now, no light entered the room.

"Poor guy," said Crewcut after a moment.

"Why?" Baldy wanted to know. "He knew what he was in for when he signed the oath."

Crewcut nodded silently.

Baldy glanced at his watch. "Should be about time."

Crewcut got his eye to the sight once again. "Lift them."

Baldy pulled the slats apart.

Crewcut could see the room now. There was movement there. He watched as Curly walked into the room and sat down at the desk opposite a heavy-set man. The deer rifle was aimed directly at Curly's face.

"There he is," said Crewcut.

Baldy nodded. "See what I told you?" He reached over and pulled the Venetian blinds upward to clear the barrel of the rifle. Then he flicked the catches and raised the lower window six inches until it, too, was above the barrel.

Crewcut watched.

"Well?" Baldy said petulantly.

"Fire?"

"Go to it."

Crewcut squeezed his finger on the trigger, and the rifle fired.

Instantly, through the sights, he could see Curly's head explode in a red cloud.

Baldy slammed the window shut, dropped the blinds, and started for the door.

"Hurry up!" he called to Crewcut.

Crewcut was right behind him when he ran out into the hallway and punched the elevator button.

The Royal Suite at the Hotel Majestic had high ceilings, gilt trim, and heavily draped windows in the fashion of the Victorian era. It took up the entire seventeenth floor of the hotel.

With Prince Tydore in the large drawing room of the suite were Police Commissioner Nolan and the Phantom. The fat little sovereign was seated comfortably in a large overstuffed chair, with Nolan and the Phantom opposite him on a couch.

The Commissioner was smoking a thin cigarillo. The Phantom wore his usual dark glasses and trench coat. The Prince was wearing a brilliant gold and blue smoking jacket and matching slippers.

"I can understand your anxiety, Commissioner," Prince Tydore was saying. "But I do have my own personal guards. It would look quite ridiculous to have dozens of policemen swarming through the halls."

Commissioner Nolan turned to the Phantom. "Well, Walker, there it is. I have a feeling the Prince is right. As I explained to you, it would have taken a great deal of persuasion for me to appropriate a proper number of guards to cover the suite. If the Prince is satisfied, so am I."

"I am not," said the Phantom. He turned to Prince Tydore. "Don't you understand that these people will stop at nothing?"

Prince Tydore shrugged. "A sovereign is always in a position of danger in a foreign country. I have faced danger before; I will face it again."

"I am not questioning your courage. Prince Tydore. I know you have a great deal. But these fanatics are absolutely determined. Believe me. They are Assassins, from an old historical cult. They are sworn to murder for profit. They will kill and kill again until they are wiped out."

"Then wipe them out," said Tydore with a faint smile.

"That is what we plan to do," said the Phantom. "But we cannot do it if you are left unprotected for one moment. It is only if you are protected that we can set a trap for the Assassins."

"You are in effect using me for bait, is that it, Mr. Walker?"

The Phantom nodded. "We must. It is the only way we can trace back to the headquarters from which these rascals operate."

"And of course where your own fiancé is now being held," Prince Tydore said slyly.

"I admit that. But since we know how these people operate, and since we know how ruthless they are, we cannot proceed unless we are assured of your protection."

"I trust my own guards, gentlemen," said Prince Tydore, turning to the Commissioner. "I hereby relieve you of any responsibility for my safety, Commissioner Nolan."

Nolan acknowledged with a nod of the head.

"It's not enough," said the Phantom. "I'm not only thinking about you but about your daughter as well. Where is she sleeping?"

Prince Tydore frowned at the Phantom. "She is sleeping in the room next to mine, sir," he said stiffly. "She is perfectly safe, I assure you. She has had royal guards around her since birth."

"But she has never been in a strange city with the Assassins after her," snapped the Phantom.

"If we can believe what you say," Prince Tydore observed remotely. "I do not like the way you cast aspersions on the courage and ability of my personal guardians."

The Phantom remained silent. He was becoming angry with his inability to sway the Prince of Tydia. Although he continued to argue, he was forming a plan in his mind. And as the plan formed, he began to feel a little more relieved of the tension which had gripped him since the attempt on the Prince's life that morning.

He knew exactly what he would do, and because he had formulated a course of action, his good cheer returned. It would not do to let either the Commissioner or the Prince know what that plan was. It would only create complications, as well as objections, in their minds.

"Well, then," he said, finally, after once again voicing all the problems he foresaw with the Prince under the surveillance of only his own men, "I suppose if you want it that way, you should have it. After all, you're the Prince."

Prince Tydore smiled. "I thought you might have forgotten that for a moment, Mr. Walker."

"Never." The Phantom smiled. He rose, turning to the Commissioner. "I suppose we should leave the Prince and Princess to their businesses, shouldn't we, Commissioner?" Nolan nodded, also rising. "Yes."

Prince Tydore's *valet de chambre*, dressed in the palace garb of Tydia, entered and bowed to the monarch.

"Telephone call for Commissioner Nolan, Your Highness."

"Plug it in here, Bardov," said Prince Tydore, pointing to a telephone jack in the wall.

The guard bowed and did as he was ordered, handing the phone to the Commissioner.

"Nolan," he barked into the phone. He listened. The Phantom waited. His own ears could make out the voice over the phone almost as easily as the Commissioner's, but he kept his face expressionless.

The Commissioner hung up, his face stern. He handed the phone to the *valet de chambre*, who took it, bowed to Prince Tydore, and backed out.

"Thank you, Bardov."

"Gentlemen," said the Commissioner, turning from .Prince Tydore to the Phantom. "I've got bad news. Someone has murdered the captured Assassin. A sniper, operating from an office building opposite the city detention wards."

"Our one lead is now destroyed," mused the Phantom.

The Commissioner's face reddened. "We'll get to the bottom of this, no matter how long it takes!" he vowed.

"Indeed," thought the Phantom, "but how long is forever?"

CHAPTER 13

When Police Commissioner Nolan and the man in the trench coat and dark glasses left Prince Tydore's suite, Bardov let them out, bowing to them discreetly as he did so.

The Commissioner, Bardov decided, was a true gentleman—a wealthy aristocratic type of the kind he was used to serving. He had worked for the Tydore family all his life in the palace at Tydia, and he knew how to recognize true royalty.

As for the man in the trench coat, Bardov was puzzled. He had seen the man's piercing eyes, and he could discern the muscular strength under the odd clothing, but he did not think he could adequately characterize him at all.

He was puzzled because he considered himself an excellent judge of character.

Shrugging, he went into Prince Tydore's drawing room and asked if there was anything else the Prince wanted. His Highness seemed a bit preoccupied and simply waved Bardov away. Bardov smiled and bowed out. He then went down the hallway and knocked on the Princess's door.

"Who is it?" she asked.

"Bardov, Your Highness," he said in Tydian.

"Come in, Bardov," said Princess Naji.

Bardov opened the door. Princess Naji lay on the bed in her

dressing gown, reading a book. She glanced up with a smile. "What is it?"

"Does Your Highness wish anything? I thought I'd retire. Of course, the regular guards are outside, if you do want anything. I'm rather tired after the excitement today."

Princess Naji smiled. "Me too, Bardov."

"Of course I understand that."

"You go right on to bed. If I need anything. I'll call the night man. We've doubled the guard, I understand."

"Yes. It's that business with the Cult of the Silken Noose,"

"An odd thing," murmured the Princess.

"Good night, then."

"Good night, Bardov."

Bardov backed out, closed the door, and went on down the hallway. His own room was at the far end of the suite.

As he passed through the central waiting room, he glanced out and saw the two guardsmen standing at the main door. He waved to them, and they grinned and waved back. They were lifelong members of the palace guard in Tydia.

Bardov walked rapidly to his room, opened the door, flicked the latch when he got inside, and strode over to the bed. He turned on the small television on the table and flipped the channels until he found a gangster movie made some thirty years ago. Bardov loved American movies, the more violent, the better. He settled back, removed his tie, jacket, and shirt, and then his shoes.

Then he lay back, his fingers laced behind his head.

He did not really hear the door to the closet open. However, a rapid movement a moment later did attract his attention, and he stiffened in surprise, his eyes wide open and mouth sagging.

"What is this—?" he gasped in Tydian.

A short, heavy-set man with an ugly face and a shock of red hair clapped his hand over Bardov's mouth, jerked hard, and pulled the Tydian *valet de chambre* off the bed, flipping him over and sending him to the floor with a jarring blow.

Bardov shook his head and tried to rise. Another blow to the head sent him reeling. He lay there, panting. He knew then that his assailant had somehow gotten into the hotel room, had hidden in the closet, and had come out to assault him.

He knew that he was at the mercy of one of the members of the Cult of the Silken Noose, which he had overheard the Commissioner and the man in the trench coat talking about with Prince Tydore that evening.

The Assassins!

Then another blow came, and Bardov blacked out.

When he came to he could hear low voices. At first he could

not understand the words, but could tell only that both voices belonged to men. Bardov became aware that his mouth was taped shut with strong pressure-sensitive tape. A gag had been thrust into his mouth so he could not make a sound. Also, his hands were tied behind his back with some kind of soft cloth, quite probably a ripped-up sheet. He had been thrust aside into one of the chairs in his room. The light was on. He could see two men by the doorway. One of them was the ugly short redhead who had attacked him. He was talking to a man much taller than he, an impressive-looking, rock-hard fellow with a shaved head and great piercing black eyes.

It was then that Bardov realized to his amazement that the redheaded man was dressed in Bardov's own clothes!

"It ain't a good fit," the redheaded man was saying to the bald giant.

"Forget it. It's good enough to fool any of the idiots in the Royal Suite." The bald man grinned evilly.

"Okay, I guess it'll have to do."

"You got the orders?"

"I think so. But you better brief me again."

"Go down the hallway to the far room on the other end. That's where the Princess Naji is sleeping. Just walk along as if you belong here. Everybody knows the *valet de chambre*. If anybody says anything, just nod and wave and keep on going as if you're on a special mission. You got that?"

"I got it."

"Okay. You get down to the last door and knock on it."

"Yeah."

"Somebody inside will probably ask you what you want. You tell her you're Bardov."

"Bardov?" The redheaded man looked over at Bardov and laughed. "Bardov."

"Right."

"Okay."

"Then you tell the Princess you have a special message for her. And she'll let you in."

"Then what?"

"This is the part where you got to do it all just right. You push against her the minute the door opens and knock her down. Slam the door behind you and pull the latch. Just before you knock on the door, you pour the ether from the bottle into the handkerchief that you've got in your pocket. When you get the Princess on the floor, push the handkerchief hard against her nose and mouth. If she struggles, slap her chin hard. Don't let her yell or breathe fresh air. In a little bit, she'll pass out."

"Okay," said the redheaded man. "I got it."

"She's out cold, and you get her on your shoulders and go over to the window and open it. There's a fire escape. Walk out onto it, climb down one flight of stairs, and climb in the room there. I'll be there, and we'll get her into the wheelchair I rented. We'll be out of the hotel in minutes, and on our way to the airport"

"Okay."

"You're going to stay here in the city. I'll take the Princess to the rendezvous spot in France, where I'll be met by Kali's man Rudd. You got that?"

"I got it."

"After that, Kali takes her to the island where the Palmer girl is."

The bald giant slapped the redhead on the shoulder and walked over to the window, which he slipped open. He stepped outside onto the fire escape and began climbing up to the next floor.

Bardov was staring through the window. They were smart, these Assassins! The bald man had rented a room above his and a room below the Princess's. There was no way to stop the kidnapping of Prince Tydore's daughter now unless Bardov got himself loose.

He tugged at his bonds.

It was useless.

He knew he couldn't get away.

The redhead heard him struggling and turned to watch him sardonically. He emptied a small bottle into a handkerchief and put the handkerchief into his jacket pocket.

"So long, jerk," he said and stepped out into the corridor, trailing the smell of ether behind him.

Bardov fought fiercely at the bonds.

Princess Naji leaned back and closed her eyes, sighing deliciously. The book she had been holding loosely in her hands fell to the bed. She let her mind wander back to those special moments during the day, those moments of high excitement and terrible fear which at the same time were replete with heady romance and unexplainable thrills.

She could see the strong face of her rescuer again and those piercing eyes behind the dark glasses. Beneath that odd costume she could imagine the tough, masculine sinews that made up his athletic body. In his face, she could read kindness and respect, qualities that few men of her acquaintance had.

If the secret were to be known, she had listened with her ear to the door panel when this stranger—he said his name was Kit Walker—had been talking with her father and the police commissioner.

He was intelligent, too. She liked the way he phrased his thoughts, liked the way his logic cut through the protocol and habit of the court and of the police system. Actually, he was the only one of the three who had really assessed the situation properly, she thought.

And yet her father had refused to listen. Even though he was Your Highness to everyone else, Prince Tydore was just "Father" to her, and he was really not all that wise when it came to judgments. Her grandfather, the King of Tydia, was the wisest of all. But of course he was old and unable to make these courtesy calls to America.

But the man Walker was the most interesting male she had met since college. She had gone to school in England, where her mother, too, had been educated. Many of the Tydores before her had attended the Sorbonne, and one had even gone to Heidelberg, but those places were out of fashion now.

Actually, she would be glad to get back to Tydia. Even though it was rather boring at the palace, she knew exactly who she was and where she was. Travel had its drawbacks. And looking after her father was not the easiest thing to do. He was a nervous, terribly frightened little man. It was Mother, the Princess Anna, who really ran the family. And Mother always told Naji that it was Naji who ran the kingdom.

Naji laughed.

There was a knock on the door. "Who is it?" she asked in Tydian.

No answer.

"Who's there?" she asked in English.

"A message for Princess Naji."

"Who was that?" she wondered. Rising, she hesitated a moment. Odd. It didn't really sound like Bardov, but he had said he was tired. Quite probably . . .

She opened the door.

Instantly, she was forced back off her feet and slammed to the floor by a blow to her head. She tried to cry out as a handkerchief was jammed into her face and nose. The blinding, eye-watering stench of ether filled her nostrils.

She kicked and scratched.

Her assailant gripped her hard, pushing down on the stifling handkerchief.

Blackness rolled in from the sides of her field of vision, and just as she was about to go under, the handkerchief was snatched from her face.

There was the sound of a solid blow directly above her,

and the man who had attacked her was lifted from her and hurled against the wall.

Princess Naji blinked, and through tear-streaming eyes, she saw that a stranger was battering the man who had assaulted her.

She rose and staggered to the bed, where she sat in dizzy nausea.

Her attacker lay still.

The other man turned and came over toward her. He towered over her, six and a half feet high, and dressed in a strange way: a skintight costume from the top of his head to his feet, a domino mask over his eyes, a belt with two guns strapped to his waist, and a tight leotard around his slender but powerful trunk.

But the eyes told her everything about him: intelligent, clear, sardonic, kindly, the eyes of her rescuer earlier in the day.

"You're coming with me. Princess Naji."

The words came out without thought. "I'd go anywhere with you. You know that."

He lifted her in his arms and held her close. "Yes. But right now you're in very great danger. Hang on tight. It's going to be a long trip."

CHAPTER 14

It had been the Phantom's decision, as soon as he had understood that Commissioner Nolan did not intend to provide police protection for the occupants of the Royal Suite, to do the job himself. His analysis of the problem revealed beyond a doubt that Princess Naji was now the prime target of the Assassins.

With that in mind, the Phantom was deep in thought when he returned to the Palmer house in the suburbs. Walking through the wooded land at the rear of the estate in his traditional Phantom costume, he let his mind wander over various alternatives for giving Naji protection.

As his logical mind eliminated the possibilities one by one, the Phantom found himself left with one course of action. He would simply have to go in and remove the Princess Naji from the suite where the Assassins knew she was staying.

And so, as night fell on the city, the Phantom hastened to the Hotel Majestic to study the means by which he might possibly gain entrance to the Princess's room. He discovered three obvious ones and a dozen not so obvious. In order of ease of accessibility, they were:

One window to the Princess's room led to a fire escape. If the window was not latched, an intruder could easily enter through it.

The front door of the Princess's room opened out onto a corridor common to the rooms of Prince Tydore, his *valet de chambre*, and the captain of the guards. This corridor was an interior corridor, and the guard outside the suite would have to be dealt with.

A back way led into the suite, used by cleaning women, repairmen, and hotel personnel. The back door was kept locked, but with the key, an intruder could easily gain access to the suite and thus the Princess's room.

There were many other possibilities, of course, some of which made use of time, of space, and of a combination of both. Thus:

1. An intruder could disguise himself as a member of the palace guard and infiltrate the rooms.

2. A disguised man could hide out for the night and effectuate a kidnapping in the early morning.

3. With the proper equipment, a daring engineer could break through the ceiling of a closet on the floor below and come up into the Princess's closet.

4. Number three, with the intruder working from the top down.

5. A second window in the Princess's room could be entered by a man climbing down the side of the outer wall.

6. An intruder could disguise himself as the hotel service man.

7. A small fire set just outside the Royal Suite could empty the rooms, letting the intruder enter and hide in the Princess's room. He could carry her off when she returned.

8. Variations on number seven: danger of the building collapsing; escape of natural gas in the pipes; poison fumes entering the air conditioning; and so on.

The Phantom concluded that he would make the simplest entry possible without making himself visible to the outside world.

He took an elevator to the top floor and stepped out into the main corridor of the hotel. At the end of the passage, he saw the sign: roof—NO ENTRY.

Glancing about him, he walked along the carpeted corridor and tried the door. It was locked. The Phantom removed a set of small lock picks from a tiny bag he carried with him, manipulated the picks and forced the door open.

Quickly he ran up the stairs and opened the door to the roof. He glanced around and saw that he was quite alone. Closing the door quietly behind him, he moved over to the edge of the building and looked down to the street below.

One of the fire escapes led down from the parapet ten feet away. Lights from the street shone up along that side of the building. He did not want to call attention to himself and so moved quickly to the center of the building where a large air-shaft had been constructed. There were windows opening out onto the air-shaft. Fire escapes went down two of the walls.

The Phantom pulled a coiled length of nylon rope from the inside pocket of his coat. Then he shed his trench coat and glasses, leaving them on the roof. Securing the nylon rope to a railing, he let himself down the side of the air-shaft with the line twisted around his shoulders in a classic rappel.

He moved swiftly and silently until he came to the seventeenth floor, where he stopped outside a darkened window. This window was not in a direct line with the Princess's bed, and he could not see what was going on inside, but he forced the latch, lifted the window and jumped inside.

It was at that moment that he heard the sound of violent struggling. He spotted a redheaded man dressed in the costume of the *valet de chambre*—obviously a disguise—trying to force a handkerchief against the Princess's mouth. The Phantom sniffed ether in the air and immediately understood.

With dispatch, he knocked the assailant away and lifted the Princess in his arms. After a few words to each other, he carried her to the window by the fire escape and opened it. He carried her down the steps quickly and stood opposite the window of the room below the Princess's room. There was no light inside.

The Phantom whispered, "We'll try this room. If I can't get the window open, we'll go down another story."

The Princess nodded.

The window opened easily. The Phantom turned and took Princess Naji's hand, helping her over the sill and into the room.

"Not a sound," he whispered. "We don't know if there's anyone in here or not."

The Phantom moved across the room toward the far end where he could see a slit of light. He turned the knob and glanced out into the hall.

It was deserted.

He grabbed the Princess's small hand in his, and the two crossed the corridor stealthily, the Phantom leading the girl toward a door that was marked FIRESTAIRS.

As the Phantom turned the knob of the fire door, he heard a sound at the other end of the corridor. Standing there by an open door was Baldy, his head gleaming in the light.

"The Phantom!" cried Baldy, quickly reaching for his jacket pocket.

The Phantom pushed the Princess in through the fire door and whispered, "Wait for me!"

He ducked behind the door frame and reached for his own handgun just as Baldy fired the first shot from his weapon. The noise racketed through the corridor as the Phantom fired back.

Baldy's second bullet smashed into the door just behind the Phantom's head. His own shot blew wood chips away from the door behind Baldy, and Baldy ducked back into the room from which he had emerged.

"Quick!" snapped the Phantom, slamming the fire door shut and grabbing the Princess. "Down we go!"

He ran down the winding stairs, carrying the Princess in his arms. She was terrified, but outwardly calm as they wound around the steep turns.

Three floors down, there was a clattering explosion in the stairwell, and a slug ricocheted back and forth in the emptiness around them.

"He's coming after us," the Phantom said to the Princess.

"I'm betting on you," smiled the Princess.

The Phantom redoubled his efforts, taking the stairs three at a time. Baldy had fired two shots, but then he began to follow and did not fire until he had hit the second landing. By that time, the Phantom had outdistanced him, taking two floors to his one.

The Phantom reached the basement and ran around the elevator banks to a supply room he had observed in his earlier exploration of the hotel building. Here, beneath one of several high windows opening out onto a service alleyway where food and supplies were delivered to the hotel during the daytime, he had hidden an extra raincoat and dark glasses for just such an emergency as this.

The Phantom rammed open the window, lifted the Princess out, and clambered up after her. Tightening the belt of the raincoat around him, the Phantom grabbed her hand and ran out toward the cross street.

A taxicab was in sight, and he hailed it quickly. Once in the cab, he called out, "International Airport."

The cab pulled away from the curb just as Baldy appeared in the alleyway, cursing.

He simply slid the handgun back into his jacket and stared hopelessly after the Phantom and the Princess in the cab.

"Bangalla," said the Phantom to the girl at the counter in the international wing at the airport. "Two round-trip tickets, please."

The girl stared at the Phantom in his trench coat and dark glasses and shrugged. She took his credit card and checked it out by phone, then returned and issued the tickets.

Meanwhile the Princess was in a phone booth nearby, waiting for the switchboard at the Hotel Majestic to connect her with her father.

"Yes," her father's voice said, finally.

"It's Naji, Dad."

"On the telephone? Why are you telephoning me?"

"I'm not at the hotel, Dad. I'm at the airport."

"The airport! Why?"

"Tonight a man tried to kidnap me. Mr. Walker rescued me. He says it's too dangerous for me to stay at the hotel. I'm going with him."

"With Mr. Walker? How do you know he isn't in with the kidnappers?"

"Oh, Dad! Don't be a fool. I know."

"When did this happen? What—?"

"Look. There's a man unconscious in my room. Have the police arrest him. He's in with the Assassins. That's what Mr. Walker told me to tell you. Do you understand?"

Pause. "Yes. I understand."

"Dad, I'll be all right. I'm going with Mr. Walker. He'll be in touch with you. You do what he says to do. So far he's been right, and no one else has. Do you hear me?"

"Uh, I hear you, Naji."

"Good-bye, Dad. We'll be in touch later."

"You're sure you're all right?"

Princess Naji sighed and hung up. The Phantom took her by the hand and led her into the area reserved for overseas passengers awaiting departure. She could see him keeping a sharp eye on the entrance to the airlines building.

But no one came to intercept them.

At the airport in Mawitaan, the capital of Bangalla, the Phantom picked up Hero, his horse, at the stables, lifted Naji onto Hero's withers and galloped out of the city and toward the Deep Woods and the Skull Cave.

CHAPTER 15

As the Phantom and the Princess sped through the depths of the jungle, the native drums were beating furiously to broadcast the arrival of the Ghost Who Walks with his beautiful companion.

Guran was ecstatic at the news. He called together the chiefs of the surrounding territories and a great feast and royal ceremony were planned. Hunters were sent out in all directions to kill wild boars and gather other delicacies fit for a king.

The Skull Cave was cleaned from top to bottom and two dozen maids of honor were brought in from the remote areas of the Great Wasteland to help prepare the feast.

And for four hours before his arrival, all the wives of the chiefs and their children were lined up along the way, standing at attention and wearing their very finest cocopalm skirts.

Soon a murmur began resounding through the jungle, and Guran, standing proudly in front of the entrance to the Skull Cave, sensed a tingle of excitement. The buzzing became louder than thousands of bees swarming on a field of sweet flowers.

"He comes! He comes! He comes!"

And then, with a clatter of hoofs, Hero, the Phantom and the Princess galloped into the clearing in front of the Skull Cave, the home of the Ghost Who Walks.

The Phantom reined up short, almost snapping Hero back on

his rear legs.

He stared down at Guran.

"Well?" His voice was like ice.

"Greetings, Phantom," said Guran with a broad smile. "Greetings, to you and your bride!"

The Phantom glowered. "It is a good thing we are speaking in Bandar and not in English. What kind of idiotic tomfoolery is this?"

The Phantom could tell that Guran had blanched, although it was particularly difficult to see it in his dark face. "But, Phantom. We have been waiting for days, and now you have come with the promised bride—"

"I am in the midst of a difficult assignment," snapped the Phantom with asperity. "Will you kindly stand out of the way while I allow the Princess Naji, of Tydia, to descend?"

"But, Phantom—" protested Guran.

"If you do not move this instant, I shall grasp you by your hair and turn you inside out as one would prepare a glove for cleaning!"

Guran gulped and moved aside.

The Phantom helped Princess Naji down from Hero's back. He spoke to her gently in English.

"Welcome to my poor abode, Princess," he said, eyeing Guran and the assembled multitude grimly. "My friends and neighbors are not used to casual visits."

"He's cute," said the Princess, smiling at Guran and leaning down to let him kiss her hand.

The Phantom watched stiffly. "Now, Guran," he said finally, waving his hand in the distance, "get all these people back to their homes, will you? We've had a long ride, and I'm hungry."

Guran nodded and withdrew diplomatically. Something was bothering the Phantom, he thought. He wondered what it could be. A lovely girl like this Princess Naji, and he didn't even want to carry her across the threshold of the Skull Cave. Obviously the Phantom's recent trip to America had unhinged him in some way. Oh, well. He would soon find out what was the matter. And then, perhaps with a little judicious and diplomatic persuasion, he could convince the Phantom that a wedding would be in the best possible interest of everyone concerned.

Wearily, he waved his arms and began ordering the thousands of people back to their homes.

Inside the Skull Cave, Princess Naji examined her surroundings in stupefaction.

"Why, it's just beautiful in here, Mr. Walker. I see you've fixed it up just like a palace. And those two skulls on either side of that— that throne—they're awfully dramatic."

The Phantom smiled. "Make yourself at home, Princess Naji.

We'll eat, and then I've got to get back to Mawitaan and America. You'll have plenty of time to explore the cave, the jungle, and acquaint yourself with the interesting customs of the natives."

He thought of Guran maliciously and allowed himself a small smile.

In a tiny cell bed in the city detention wards, the redheaded prisoner lay on his cot, staring at the ceiling. He could not yet understand what had happened in the abortive attempt to kidnap the Princess Naji from the Royal Suite of the Hotel Majestic.

Everything had been going like clockwork, and suddenly—boom! A strange figure dressed in a skintight leotard had descended on him, smashed him into the wall, and left him there unconscious. When he had come to, he had been staring up into the eyes of a pair of Prince Tydore's Palace Guards.

Then, after frightening hours of inquisition and interrogation, he had been brought to this impenetrable cell.

He counted back and remembered that he had been here at the city jail for over two days now. He wondered how long it would take to bring him to trial. He knew that he had been questioned many times about Kali and the Cult, but he had been able to resist and had said nothing so far.

Somehow the police knew the identity of his own co-conspirator—they called him "Baldy"—but they had not caught him. He wondered if Baldy had gotten to the Princess after he had run out of the hotel. Probably not.

He held out no hope for the future. He knew that the rule of the Assassins was not to talk, not to hope, and not to live. Somehow they would find him and kill him. After these last few days, that would be a pleasure.

"Hey, Red!" cried the guard.

He turned and smiled. The guard, who called himself Jess Boynton, was a jovial roly-poly fellow who liked to joke with the prisoners. "Red," of course, referred to the prisoner's hair. The prisoner had never revealed his name; on pain of death, he had been warned not to by the Assassins.

"Almost time for chow," said Boynton.

"I could use a bite to eat," said Red in his slightly accented English.

"What's new with you?" Boynton asked.

It amused the guard to pretend that there might be something new with Red.

"Nothing."

Boynton broke into long peals of laughter. "Not a bad setup for chow," he said. "Linguini."

"What's linguini?" Red asked.

"Beautiful food!" said Boynton. "You don't like Italian food?"

"When are you going to bring it in?" Red asked.

"Few minutes." He stood by the bars and peered in. "Hey, Red. There's still no news of that Princess you tried to snatch. Whoever beat you up got away clean. How do you like them apples?"

Red frowned, wondering what apples had to do with princesses.

"Huh?"

"The story goes in the newspapers that a kidnapping plot against the Princess Naji of Tydia was foiled by the capture of the kidnapper. However, another news story then got out that the Princess has vanished! Either she's hiding out, or she's been kidnapped by someone else."

Red's ears pricked up. Hope formed in his heart. If Baldy had indeed succeeded in picking up the trail of Princess Naji, perhaps she had been taken to Kali.

"What do you think of that, Red?"

"It's a shame, isn't it?" he said.

"What? That you didn't kidnap her and get the money?"

Red smiled. "Yes."

The guard began whispering. "Red, let me give you a piece of advice. You've been clamming up to the authorities, you know? I mean, you haven't told them nothing about who's hired you, and all that. I got word from the grapevine today that if you drop a name, they'll let you off with a nice easy sentence. Otherwise they're going to throw the book at you."

Red was baffled. First he was baffled by the idea of a grapevine growing in the city jail. And after that he was exceedingly puzzled at the idea of somebody tossing a book at him. He was trying to figure out what it all meant when Jess sighed.

"I'm telling you, Red, if you spill the beans, they'll let you off the hook!"

String beans? wondered Red. Or green beans? Or pork and beans? And what was that about a hook? He didn't like the sound of that.

"Talk!" Boynton said. "You hear me? You'll be a free man! They're after the biggies, not you."

Red stared at Boynton. "If I tell who I was working with, they'll let me off lightly?"

"That's it, Red!"

Red frowned. Possibly Boynton was not lying to him. He might even be paid by the authorities to spread the word that a fix was in.

Yes. He would talk. Once they called him . . .

"Be back in a sec with the chow, Red. Sit tight!"

Red climbed back on his bunk and lay there with his hands laced behind his head. For the first time in two days, he felt hope. Indeed, if he could simply say a few words, and they did let him go, he knew a little hideout where he could stay, far from the probing eyes of Kali.

What would Kali do for him if he kept his mouth shut? Nothing.

And if he could get away, he had many more good years to go. Baldy hadn't helped him at all the night of the kidnapping. What did he owe to any of them?

His eyes closed.

A little place out in the Southwest desert, far from prying eyes. He could live like a king. . . .

He heard the rattle of the cup on the bar.

"Chow!"

He got up, smiling, and walked over toward the door where the food came in through a small slot. He'd talk, and he'd tell them.

"Eat hearty."

He recognized the voice.

He looked up.

The bald gleaming head was the last thing he saw. That, and the flicker of malice in the black eyes and the smirk on the wide mouth.

The explosion of the gunshot shattered the confines of the cell. The force of the bullet in his heart drove him back against the bunk and almost broke his back before he toppled to the floor bleeding his life out.

CHAPTER 16

The Phantom was waiting in line to clear customs at International Airport when a man in a gray suit and striped tie approached him.

"Your bags will be taken care of, Mr. Walker. Will you come with me, please?"

The Phantom studied him a moment. The man had the hard-eyed look of a career cop and the no-nonsense attitude of an uncorruptible civil servant.

"Of course," he said politely.

"This way."

The gray-suited man led him out through a rear door marked no admittance, which proved to be a passageway leading to still another door, this one opening out into the night. A narrow paved roadway led by the side of the building, and a limousine was parked there with the lights on and the motor idling.

With the exception of the driver, the Phantom could not see who was inside. All the windows were covered with dark curtains.

"If you please." The gray-suited man opened the rear door of the limousine and indicated that the Phantom should enter.

The Phantom ducked into the car and found himself sitting next to Police Commissioner Nolan.

"Thank you for your cooperation, Mr. Walker," said Nolan

with a faint smile.

The man in the gray suit slipped into the driver's seat.

"All right, Harders," Nolan called to him.

The limousine moved along the street, turned a corner, and started down a gently sloping ramp toward a traffic artery.

"What's this all about, Commissioner?" the Phantom asked.

"Prince Tydore was reluctant to press charges," said Nolan in his tight-lipped fashion, staring straight ahead. "We won't be holding you. In fact, he expressed the wish that I drive you directly to him."

The Phantom thought about Nolan's statement. "Charges?" he asked. "What charges?"

"Charges of kidnapping Princess Naji, Mr. Walker Kidnapping is, of course, illegal."

"I?"

"You."

"I interrupted an attempt to kidnap the Princess," the Phantom corrected the Commissioner.

"You carried her off. You were seen bundling her into a cab in front of the Hotel Majestic."

"She went of her own free will."

"Prince Tydore did not know about her decision," Nolan said, tight-faced.

"I'll explain to him," said the Phantom harshly.

"Mr. Walker, we live in this land by the stringent observance of law and order. I don't know what kind of laws you have where you come from. Here, it is mandatory to cooperate with the people chosen by the community to enforce the laws."

"I removed the Princess Naji from a site where I thought she would be unsafe," the Phantom said.

"In effect, you kidnapped her."

"Nevertheless, my aim was to protect her."

"I suppose, in your own mind, you think you did right." "You would not reinforce the guards placed on the Royal Suite."

"Yes. And I told you why."

"I was acting in the Princess's best interests."

The Commissioner shrugged. Then he said: "Because of you, another man in our custody has been killed."

"Who?"

"The would-be kidnapper of the Princess."

"How was he killed?"

"Someone assumed the identity of one of our turnkeys and shot him in his cell."

"Have you identified the killer?"

"He escaped. He was dressed, as I said, like a guard, and he simply walked away after the killing. The corpse was not discovered for a good ten minutes."

"You can't hold me responsible for that!"

"Of course not. I am not doing so. But I'm not forgetting that since you've been in our city, two men have been killed while in custody."

"The Assassins have a stringent rule. When one of their members is captured by the law, he either takes his own life, or is dispatched by another member of the cult."

"None of us were aware of this."

"I read up on it during my trip home with the Princess."

The Commissioner turned now, and his eyes were dark. "Where is your home?"

"In a remote sector of the world, Commissioner. I assure you it would do no good to name the place. It is not on any map."

"And while there you researched the habits of the Assassins, as you call these people?"

The Phantom nodded.

The Commissioner plunged his hands into the pockets of his coat and slouched down in the seat. "Perhaps we shall have to rethink our plan of attack."

The Phantom smiled. "Exactly what I have been studying." He hesitated. "Our primary mission is still to find and release Diana Palmer."

Nolan grunted. "There has been no further word from the Palmer residence."

"Then obviously no more ransom notes have been delivered." The Phantom could feel his hands growing cold. "Perhaps Kali and his men have done away with her."

"Not likely. The way I read this mob—or cult as you call it—is this: they're after money. They'll hang onto her until they get the money. They're hidden somewhere, and very well hidden. There's been no sign yet of that hijacked airliner."

"I assume they're trying to work the Tydore kidnapping now. They've failed in two attempts to collect ransom—in Diana's kidnapping, and in the aborted attempt on Princess Naji."

"Who's next?"

"It's obvious. Prince Tydore himself."

Commissioner Nolan sank back in the seat again. "I could fortify Prince Tydore's guards by adding city police."

The Phantom smiled thinly. "You've finally come around to admitting I was right in the first place."

"Perhaps."

"I'm going to surprise you, Commissioner. I'm going to recommend that you not do that."

Nolan blinked.

"It's obvious that the more of Kali's men we capture, the more corpses we're going to have on our hands."

"I see what you're getting at."

"Let's play it another way."

"How's that?"

The Phantom gathered his thoughts together, frowned, and began to phrase them verbally.

A small portable transmitter had been set up against the outside wall of a small, grubby room near the North River docks. An electric line from the roof antenna had been hooked into the set near the back. A small table stood in the middle of the room; folding chairs were stacked against a wall. A pair of suitcases were placed against the wall, and in the closet, the door of which was open, hung several sets of clothes. One of the suits was the uniform of a detention guard. Three others in view had the bright epaulettes of the royal guard of Prince Tydore.

The outer door opened, a hand sneaked in, switched on the light, and two men came in, panting from the long walk upstairs.

"Bah!" snapped the big bald-headed man. "Three flights up and I'm dead!"

Crewcut pulled one of the folding chairs from the wall, set it up, and slumped in it. "I'm beat."

"What a crummy place," Baldy growled, glancing around.

A large rat, startled by the slam of the door and the voices of the two men, scuttled along the floor molding, turning its head once to focus its gleaming red eyes on the human intruders.

"Yeow!" screeched Crewcut. "A rat!"

Baldy cursed. "Beat it, rat!" He stared right back at the beady red eyes.

The rat grimaced—an expression Baldy took to be a malevolent grin—-and moved sedately along to the corner where two moldings came together in a bad carpenter's joint. He pushed his nose into the crack at the joint and vanished behind the wall.

"We've got to wrap up this job and get out of here," snapped Crewcut. "I don't like this setup one bit."

"Come on," chided Baldy. "You're a big boy now. You're an Assassin. Assassins don't cry, do they?"

"Shut up, you hairless freak. You don't like it any better than I do."

"No, I don't, but until we show some results, we're stuck here. So let's get moving."

Crewcut gazed at the portable transmitter. "Wait till Sheik-al-Jabal gets the bill for that little beauty. We'll all be looking for jobs."

Baldy snorted. "The police confiscated the other unit. It was getting untrustworthy, anyway. Now where's that list of names you got from our contact in Canada?"

Crewcut handed a sheet over to Baldy, who looked at it carefully. "Six. That ought to do the trick. I suppose they'll be here any minute."

Ten minutes later there was a series of knocks on the door—one short, two longs, and a short.

Baldy opened the door.

A stoop-shouldered, powerful-looking, piratical character entered. He had squint eyes, a mop of black hair that hung over his ears, and was dressed in a seaman's high-necked shirt and deck pants.

"I'm Damon," he said, giving one of the code names written on the sheet of paper. Baldy nodded. "The rest will be coming."

Soon five other nondescript thugs entered the little room, and Baldy surveyed them with satisfaction.

"Okay. You take orders from me. That's all you need to know. We've got the uniforms here in the closet." Baldy gestured to the half-open door. "Each one of you knows exactly what to do. You just get in that suite and get rid of one of the guards already there and take his place. I don't care how you work it out, just so long as you do it. Any questions?"

No one had any.

"That's it, then. Get yourself a uniform from the closet and split."

In five minutes the six cutthroats had left, each carrying one of the uniforms Baldy had stolen from Prince Tydore's royal luggage.

Crewcut sat down in front of the transmitter. He switched on the warm-up toggle.

Baldy sighed. "All right. Let's see how we word this one. We won't call it Failure Number Two. We'll say Plan Two is over. Now for Plan Three." He closed his eyes and shuddered. "No matter what we say, Kali will hit the ceiling."

CHAPTER 17

Sheik-al-Jabal Hara Kali arose and donned the sacred blood-red ceremonial robe of the Cult of the Silken Noose, observed himself in the mirror with satisfaction, inserted a cigarette in his ivory holder, and walked out of his bedroom into the dining room of the palace.

It was early, and even though he knew it was nighttime on the other side of the globe where his cultists were working, he hastened across the sandy tropical yard to the small radio shack which had been built on the highest point of the promontory so that its antenna could pick up the most remote signals with ease.

The turbaned radio operator glanced up at Kali peering in through the doorway.

"Have we received a message from America?"

"None," responded the operator.

Kali puffed on his cigarette furiously. Behind the monocle his eye glinted with frustration. Three full days since he had received half a message, and that one broken off in the middle. Fools! They were trained to cope with emergencies. Why hadn't they fixed the set or purchased a new one? They had the proper credit cards and a blanket authorization to use them if necessary.

It occurred to him again that total disaster might have struck, that all of them might have been imprisoned. But that was highly unlikely. There were too many of them in position in America.

Someone could have—would have—gotten through to him by radio.

No, this was a momentary setback, that was all. But what was worrying him was the lack of money for future operations. Without the Palmer money, the Tydore operation was overextending their credit. And without the Tydore money—and that quickly—the operation at the White House would have to wait. And that was the culmination of the present phase of operations.

Kali swept past the courtyard where Toto, the gorilla, sat chained to the wall.

The big beast leaped up and down and beat on his chest as Kali passed, grimacing at him. Kali knew the beast hated cigarette smoke. It apparently stirred some atavistic instinct against forest fires in his intelligence centers, and he blew a cloud at him maliciously. Toto banged on the ground and jumped back against the stone wall, howling.

In a few moments, Kali was passing through the dungeon section of the castle. When he came to the barred door, he saw Diana Palmer standing there.

Her hair was disheveled, and her dress was wrinkled. Even though her face had been washed with the water he had grudgingly offered her the night before, she seemed somewhat untidy. It was obvious that, confined to the cell, she could not take care of her grooming, but that was her problem, not his.

"You brute," Diana began. "When are you going to let me out of here?"

"When the money is paid, Miss Palmer, and not one instant sooner!"

"I hope my uncle never pays you!" snapped Diana in a fit of temper.

"I'm not blaming you, Miss Palmer," said Kali smoothly, "but I do wish your people would act."

"I don't understand why they haven't tried to contact you."

Kali did not inform her thwart his own communications system had broken down completely, preventing him from sending any more ransom instructions.

"Nor do I, Miss Palmer."

Tears started to gather in Diana's eyes. She blinked them away. "I beg of you to let me out in the sunshine today. Would you please?"

Kali frowned. "Perhaps."

"You promised me the first day, and the second, and you broke your promises. But you've simply got to let me out. I'm withering away in here."

He liked her spirit, but at the present time he couldn't bother with spirit. He simply had to make some progress on the negotiations. He turned his back on her and puffed away in self-contempt.

"Are you going to let me walk today?" Diana demanded.

"I'll think about it," Kali said darkly.

"If this cult of yours had any decency, it wouldn't allow you to torture human beings the way you do."

Kali turned on her, his lips drawn back into a thin line. "Our cult is one of the oldest in the modern Western world, Miss Palmer. The phase through which we are presently passing is a dangerous one. This is the phase of rebuilding toward the glorious days! We fully intend to remake the entire Western world over into the image of paradise."

"Humph," snorted Diana. "You sound like some kind of nut."

"The cult of assassination is merely the first phase of our plan to dominate the world with enlightenment, scientific knowledge, and eternal justice."

"A fine way to start—kidnapping people," muttered Diana. "Budgetary problems have made it necessary, Miss Palmer," mused Kali. "Some day you will thank your lucky stars for having helped us toward our goal." Kali puffed on his cigarette and gazed at the high square window, his voice exultant. "We will form a society superior to any other in the history of the world."

Diana shook her head.

"O Jabal, O Kali," a voice sounded outside the castle.

Kali straightened. "The radio operator." He turned to Diana. "Perhaps this is your lucky day, my dear."

The static on the set was horrendous, but Kali could hear the faint voice of his American malik:

"... reporting, Sheik-al-Jabal! Can you hear me?"

"Yes, yes," snapped Kali, leaning over the operator's shoulder and grabbing the microphone. "Will you please tell me what has been happening?"

"A great . . ." The voice faded. ". . . and then of course—"

"Stop, stop!" growled Kali. "Go back over that, will you? I didn't hear."

"Oh. The ransom in the Palmer affair was not delivered, Jabal. The Phantom tried to destroy us, but he failed."

"Who was that?"

"The Phantom. The Ghost Who Walks."

"Say that again?"

"The Ghost Who Walks—an avenging spirit."

Kali cursed to himself. "Go on, go on! We'll straighten this all out later."

"The police found the transmitter, and we had to purchase another. In the meantime, we proceeded to the second affair—the Tydore kidnapping.

"Yes, yes."

"Unfortunately, through excessive zeal of the authorities, we were unable to bring the Princess to our secret airport for delivery to the island. Therefore—"

Kali groaned. "Where is the Princess now?"

"She has vanished. We are now about to threaten Prince Tydore and kidnap him if he refuses to pay the ransom."

"Do not fail again, Malik, or I will have you replaced."

"Yes, sire."

"Now who is this Phantom you have been jabbering about?"

"We suspect he was likewise responsible for the disappearance of the Princess after we failed to kidnap her."

"Eliminate him. Do you have to be told every step to take?"

"He is a difficult man to eliminate," the voice complained. "We have tried everything. Some say he is simply a spirit and not a human being at all."

"You superstitious fools! Do I have to come back to America, and do it for you?"

"We will succeed, never fear, sire."

"You had better," grumbled Kali.

"We will be contacting Prince Tydore tonight, sire."

"Good. Have you infiltrated his guards?"

"That move is now in the works. We will deliver the note tonight."

"Very well. If he balks, move on to Phase Three."

"Yes, sire. That is, kidnap him and take him to the secret airport for transshipment to the island."

"Exactly. Now let's go back to the Palmer affair."

"Yes?"

"Deliver another ransom note. Set up the meet for any place you want, but make this one work. If you don't get the money tonight, I'll put out an order to assassinate both the Palmers—mother and uncle. There will be repercussions if this happens, as you well know."

"Sire, must we—?"

"You must! If you fail to get the ransom, they will have to be eliminated. Now set up a successful exchange and get the money. We are in dire need of funds to move toward *l'Affaire de la Maison Blanche.*"

"The what?"

"Oh, forget it."

"We'll work it out, sire. Is that all for now?"

"Yes," hissed Kali. "Now, you bungling fools, move and don't commit any more silly mistakes!"

"We committed no mistakes," howled the voice. "It was the Phantom who made our hands falter, made our eyes blur, made our hearts fail."

"Shut up, you quivering idiots! It's your own incompetence that's ruining our affairs, not anything from the outside."

"The Phantom, sire—"

"Good-bye!"

Sheik-al-Jabal Hara Kali pulled the plug of the microphone out of the control panel and handed it to the startled operator.

Then Kali stomped off across the sand to the castle basement where he stared at Diana Palmer a moment in ugly silence.

"You'd better start saying whatever prayers you know, Miss Palmer. We're going to try again to get that money from your people. If it isn't forthcoming immediately, I'll have to get rid of you."

Diana Palmer turned pale.

"And I'll have to kill your mother and uncle, too. They know too much about us."

"Please, no!" cried Diana.

"Just pray. It's your only hope."

Kali spun on his heel and stalked off through the dank corridors of the ancient castle dungeon.

CHAPTER 18

Stepping off the elevator on the seventeenth floor of the Hotel Majestic, the Phantom adjusted his dark glasses and trench coat carefully and strolled along the corridor to the Royal Suite.

The plan he had outlined to Police Commissioner Nolan was characteristically simple and to the point: since the police were not going to guard Prince Tydore, the Phantom would do so himself. And if there was a ransom note or a telephone call, the Phantom would take care of that, too. There were several options open.

Nolan had agreed to let the Phantom take over, but not without some hesitation. However, the Phantom could be persuasive when he wished to be, and he had won over the Commissioner without excessive argument.

The royal guards straightened when the Phantom appeared at the door to the Royal Suite.

"I'd like to see Prince Tydore, please," said the Phantom.

"I'm sorry. He's not receiving visitors."

The guards were both husky brutes, the Phantom noticed. The speaker had no accent whatsoever. If anything, he spoke rather uneducated English. The Phantom studied him carefully, without seeming to, and then turned his attention to the other guard.

Both ignored him.

"Tell him Mr. Walker is here," said the Phantom. "He's expecting me."

The second guard cleared his throat. "We've been told no one is to come in tonight," he said in a surly tone.

"I see."

The Phantom realized that the guards were impostors. Prince Tydore's men were by no means sophisticated gentlemen, but they were at least presentable. These two uniformed men struck the Phantom as thugs. He recalled Nolan's story about the murderer who had infiltrated the detention ward in a fake uniform. If these two were Assassins pretending to be guards of Prince Tydore . . .

"Please tell Prince Tydore I called, if you will?" the Phantom said politely and rang for the elevator. When it came, he stepped inside, glancing once out at the two guards who were watching him, and pressed the button for the sixteenth floor.

There he stepped out and walked to the end of the corridor where a window looked out over the city. He knew that there was no fire escape leading to Prince Tydore's window, but there was one leading to Princess Naji's.

However, when he opened the window, he discovered that the facade of the building was composed of large slabs of rock at least a foot long and two feet wide. Between these rock slabs there were indentations an inch deep. The Phantom could easily scale such a wall, using the tremendous strength of his fingers to cling to the rock slabs as if they were steps.

Quickly glancing around to make sure the coast was clear, he slipped out of his trench coat, hat and glasses, and climbed out through the open window. Gripping the ledge of the windowsill with one hand, he closed the window with the other.

Then he lowered himself carefully down the wall, gripped the edges of the stone slabs and began moving around the side of the building toward the room under Prince Tydore's.

It was very dark out, with a light fog hanging in the air. He could not see down into the street below; he hoped no one was watching him.

Finally he had crossed the wall to a point directly below the Prince's room. Then he began moving up the wall, holding on with his hands until his feet found a toehold, and then holding on with one hand while the other explored to find the next hand grip.

Hanging onto the sill of the window to the Prince's room, he pulled himself up to chest level. He could see Prince Tydore inside the room, leaning back despondently in an overstuffed chair near his bed. The Prince of Tydia was dressed in his royal blue robe and turban. It was obvious that he was alone.

With his fingernail, the Phantom tapped on the window several times, and finally the Prince roused himself from his stupor long enough to see the Phantom's silhouette at the window.

He rose with alacrity and pulled open the window. "Who the devil are you?"

"I'm Mr. Walker, Prince Tydore. I've come to help you. I couldn't get in the front way."

"Mr. Walker! Where's my daughter?"

The Phantom slipped into the room and closed the window quickly, making as little noise as possible. He put his finger to his lips and spoke in a low voice.

"I've taken her where she will be completely safe. Don't worry about her. You're the one that the gang is after now."

"What is this costume you're wearing?" Prince Tydore asked, reaching out to touch the skintight suit.

"It makes it easier for me to get around to help those who need help."

Prince Tydore sighed dolefully. "I guess I'm one of those, all right. But how can you help me?" Prince Tydore wrung his hands in dismay. "I'm surrounded by the henchmen of those kidnappers. My guards have all been replaced by armed killers. I have no hope."

"There's always hope," said the Phantom. "Now you just let me take care of this. What exactly happened to your guards?"

"The cutthroats apparently replaced them one by one. I have no one I can trust now."

The Phantom considered. "Have the kidnappers contacted you in any way yet?"

"No," wailed the fat little man.

"They will," the Phantom said with assurance. "Meanwhile, I think we should forget all this and enjoy a little game of chess. Do you play?"

Prince Tydore's face lit up. "But of course!"

In the middle of a Sicilian Defense, the telephone on the Prince's stand rang.

"That's my private line," said Prince Tydore, his face wet with perspiration.

"Answer it," ordered the Phantom. "It's the Assassins."

With shaking fingers the Prince of Tydia lifted the telephone. "Hello?"

"Prince Tydore?" a voice rasped on the other end of the line.

The Phantom could distinguish the words clearly with his exceptionally keen hearing.

"Yes."

"You can't escape. I guess you know that now." The voice chuckled.

"Who is this?" Prince Tydore asked, trying to summon up a modicum of courage.

"You know who this is!" snapped the voice. "Now be quick. We have no time to lose."

"But I don't know what you—"

"We want ten million dollars' worth of your royal jewels, or we'll kidnap you and hold you for a far larger ransom." There was a pause. "Prince Tydore?"

"Yes?" The monarch could barely speak.

"Do you hear me? We can kidnap you. Your own guards are under lock and key. They belong to us."

"But I haven't any jewels," Prince Tydore protested in a trembling voice.

"We know all about you," snapped the would-be kidnapper. "We know your jewels are listed at twenty to thirty millions by the insurance companies. We know the Princess always wears them at functions outside Tydia. We know you carry them with you in a private safe. Now get those jewels ready to be picked up by us or prepare to be carried off!"

There was a slam as the caller hung up.

Gingerly Prince Tydore replaced the phone.

"You heard?" he asked the Phantom in a tormented voice.

"I heard," the Phantom assured him grimly. He looked around hurriedly. "Where are the jewels?"

Prince Tydore put his head in his hands. "They'll kill me! I know they will!"

"Don't think about it," said the Phantom. "If you have the jewels, they know it. Do you have them?"

"Yes. Hidden. Well guarded."

"Good." The Phantom frowned, thinking furiously. "Their intelligence is first-rate. Obviously they can't get at the jewels themselves, but need you to bring them out. Now there'll be another telephone call, informing you when and where to deliver the jewels."

"I'll—I'll get them ready—"

The Phantom held up a hand. He shook his head. "No. Don't touch them. They may be watching to see where you go. I've got an idea—"

Prince Tydore blinked. "But they said they'd kidnap me Mr. Walker! I don't want to be held hostage. They may kill me. After all, it's only a bag of jewels. They can have them."

"Nonsense! If you turn them over, you'll encourage these ruffians. Don't you understand, you've got to stand up to them."

"How? How can I stand up to them?"

The phone rang again.

The Phantom pointed to it.

"Hello," Prince Tydore said hesitantly.

"Put the jewels in a pillowcase. You got that?"

Prince Tydore's eyes widened. He looked at the Phantom helplessly. The Phantom nodded, encouraging the Prince to answer in the affirmative.

"Yes. I understand."

"Ten million dollars' worth, Prince Tydore. If you don't come up with the right amount, we'll take you somewhere you won't want to be. You'll be lucky ever to see Tydia again. Do you hear me?"

"Yes."

"Get the jewels into the pillow slip, tie it up, and put the pillow slip on the window ledge. Do you understand?"

Prince Tydore nodded. "Yes."

"You've got five minutes."

"Is that all?" Prince Tydore wailed.

"Leave it on the window ledge. If you try to alert the authorities, you'll wish you hadn't. You hear me?"

"Yes," said Prince Tydore in a tremulous voice.

The phone slammed down.

Prince Tydore rose and faced the Phantom indecisively. "I'll get the jewels, Mr. Walker."

"No, you won't," said the Phantom. He walked quickly over to the large bed, removed a pillow, and slid the pillowcase from it. It was spacious, and the Phantom stuffed a number of jars and cut-glass ornaments from a bureau into it.

"What are you doing?" Prince Tydore asked.

"I'm filling up the pillowcase with whatever you have lying around. Are there any books here? I haven't got enough weight yet."

"But—"

The Phantom found some books in a small bookcase against the wall and dumped them into the case. Finally it was heavy enough, and he twisted the top together, tying it with a string.

"What are you doing that for?"

"I want to see exactly how they're going to remove this from the window. If that's what they're going to do. It may be a bluff."

"I see. But—"

"No buts about it, Prince Tydore."

Prince Tydore sighed. "I don't mind telling you, I'm scared to death!"

"Don't be," the Phantom said reassuringly.

He took the pillowcase over to the window ledge and set it there, glancing out into the night as he did so.

"All right," he told Prince Tydore. "We go right back where

we were and wait."

It was very quiet in the room. The Phantom turned down all the lights but one and raised his finger for silence.

In exactly five minutes, there was movement at the window. A large metal hook on the end of a silken line was slowly lowered into view at the top of the window opening.

"That's it," whispered the Phantom. "They're on the roof, or somewhere above us in the hotel, lowering that hook on a rope. They'll pull up the pillowcase. Well, Prince Tydore, we know they're capable of getting away with it, don't we?"

"Yes," said Prince Tydore faintly.

"Buck up," said the Phantom. "We aren't licked yet."

"But when they discover what's in the bag—"

The Phantom was watching the hook as it caught in the neck of the pillowcase and straightened up. The pillowcase swung out from the windowsill, vanished below a moment, and then slowly rose, swaying back and forth until it was out of sight.

The Phantom moved over to the window and looked up the side of the building. He could see nothing. As he waited there, he could hear a cry of rage in the distance. Then, quite suddenly the empty pillowcase flew out from the roof and began falling down the side of the building.

The Phantom pulled in his head and watched it drift by.

"Now we make our move."

Prince Tydore was almost in tears. "What do we do now? They're coming down here to kidnap me."

The Phantom smiled. "Yes. And that fits in very well with our plans."

"They do? What are our plans?"

"I need your turban, Prince Tydore," he said suddenly. "And your robe, if I may?"

Prince Tydore blinked. "But, Mr. Walker. This is my royal robe. Only I am permitted to wear it. The same is true of my turban—"

The Phantom straightened. "While I put them on, Your Highness," he said firmly, "you get into the closet. Don't you see? They're coming down to get you. And when they get here, we'll have the lights out. I'll be in that bed of yours, and they've got to think I'm Prince Tydore. I need your robe and turban so they'll kidnap me."

Prince Tydore blinked and his lips trembled.

The Phantom pushed him toward the closet and opened the door. "Your turban. Your Highness. If you please. And your robe?"

"Well," said the Prince. He didn't like it, but he complied.

The Phantom twisted the turban expertly around his head,

got into the Prince's royal blue robe, and made for the phone. Quickly he dialed and waited for the voice at the other end, which was Police Commissioner Nolan's private home line.

"Yes?" It was Nolan, slightly sleepy, slightly testy.

"Plan B is in action," said the Phantom.

"What's Plan B?" grumbled the Commissioner.

"I'm taking Prince Tydore's place," the Phantom explained quickly. "The guards have been replaced here, as we suspected. I think they'll clear out once I'm gone. Make sure you take care of the Prince."

"Yes, yes," said the Commissioner. "And thanks, Mr. Walker."

"I'd suggest you diplomatically send His Excellency and his entourage back to his native land."

"And you?"

"Don't worry about me. At last I'm on Diana Palmer's trail."

In minutes the Phantom was lying on the bed, with the lights in the room turned off. All he could hear were the sounds of the city outside.

It had to work, he thought. If not . . .

CHAPTER 19

Three men crouched behind the roof parapet of the Hotel Majestic. Two of them were the Assassins known to the Phantom as Baldy and Crewcut. The third was a tall man with a heavy, well-built body and an extremely small head. In shape, he resembled a clothespin.

"The Prince thinks he's pulling a fast one," said Baldy spitefully. "I had an idea he would try something like this."

"What do we do now?" Crewcut asked.

"We climb down to Prince Tydore's room and kidnap him." Baldy snapped his fingers. "The rope, stupid."

Crewcut gathered up the rope that had been used to haul up the pillowcase full of trinkets and books and handed it to Baldy.

"I'll go down first," Baldy announced. "You follow."

"What about me?" asked Pinhead.

"You stay up here and pull in the rope. I don't want any evidence lying around."

"Then what?"

"Go downstairs the same way we came up. Get in the car. Pull it around to the rear of the hotel. We'll come out through the back door. I want that car revved up and ready to split when we do."

"Right," said Pinhead.

Baldy lowered the rope until the end of it hung just below Prince Tydore's window. Then he made sure it was carefully knotted to one of the vent pipes near the parapet.

"Wait till I get into the room, and then you follow me," he told Crewcut.

With that, he let himself down over the parapet, grasped the rope, and climbed down knot by knot until he came to the window of the Royal Suite on the seventeenth floor.

He let himself in quietly, peering through the gloom of the darkened room to see if he could distinguish the Prince. He saw a form on the bed. Jerking on the rope, he signaled Crewcut to follow.

In a moment, Crewcut stood in the room with him. The rope vanished, hauled up to the roof by Pinhead.

Baldy put his finger to his lips and tiptoed over to the bed. The form dressed in turban and robe lay there quietly.

"It's the Prince," Baldy assured Crewcut. "He's so scared he's gone to bed. Have you got that ether?"

Crewcut brought out a bottle, opened it and soaked a , handkerchief with its contents, then recapped it. The odor of ether spread through the room.

"Hurry up," whispered Baldy, "before it puts us to sleep."

Crewcut moved quickly to the bed, grabbed the sleeping form, and covered the mouth and nose with the handkerchief. There was a brief struggle, and then the form went limp.

"Good," said Baldy. He pulled an empty laundry bag from inside his sweatshirt and quickly opened it. "You know what to do," he told Crewcut.

Crewcut lifted the sleeping form from the bed while Baldy held the laundry bag open. Soon the man was inside the large bag, snoring gently.

Baldy pulled the strings tightly around the lip of the bag and tied them together in a knot.

The two men lifted the bag, opened the door to the Prince's room, and moved quickly out into the drawing room. Baldy pointed to the left. They carried the laundry bag toward the tradesman's entrance to the Royal Suite.

In a moment they were descending in the service elevator. Without stopping, the elevator traveled all the way to the basement. When the doors opened, Baldy and Crewcut carried the laundry bag out into the basement corridor and went toward the rear of the hotel.

In moments they were in the alleyway, where a car awaited them, the engine purring softly.

"Good boy," said Baldy with satisfaction.

The door opened, and they tossed the laundry bag inside. Crewcut got in the back. Baldy joined Pinhead in the front seat.

"What happens to the guys we got for guards?" Crewcut asked as the car started up and left the alleyway.

"Their assignment ends at midnight," said Baldy. "I expect they'll leave the easiest way they can."

"But won't that alert the real guards?"

"Sure," said Baldy. "But then it'll be too late. We've got the Prince."

Crewcut nodded. "I don't know why you went to all that trouble to infiltrate Prince Tydore's guards when we were able to pull the kidnapping off without their help."

"Window-dressing," said Baldy. "We had to get the Prince into a state of panic before he'd give up the jewels."

"But he didn't give up the jewels."

Baldy grunted. "That's the way the ball bounces." He cheered up. "Anyway, we got him out of there, and Kali will be happy to see him."

Pinhead drove up to a signal and stopped. "Why didn't you use the guards to help you?"

Baldy stared at the driver insolently. "We couldn't let them know we snatched the Prince."

"Why not?"

"They'd blackmail us to the end of our days. You never trust a man you hire—especially a professional cutthroat!"

Pinhead shrugged and the car started up. Traffic had thinned. They were driving along the riverfront. The cool breeze blew in off the water. Soon they came to the cluttered area where the North River docks began.

The car pulled up beside a deserted warehouse surrounded by piles of crates and boxes.

Baldy opened the car door. Crewcut pushed out the laundry bag, and the two men carried it across the cleared area to a small beat-up jetty. A powerboat, bobbing gently in the river current, was moored there.

In moments, they were gliding over the water, carrying the laundry bag in the bottom of the boat.

The Phantom opened his eyes, but could see absolutely nothing. His head throbbed from the effects of the ether. He was hot in the stuffy bag.

He remembered the moment the crewcut Assassin had shoved the ether-saturated handkerchief into his face. He had not struggled at all, but had succumbed deliberately. And that was the last he had known.

The large cloth bag in which he had been tied up was sturdy and very difficult to move about in. The Phantom knew that he should not make a sudden movement because it might alert someone on guard over him.

However, as he lay there, he could hear only the steady drone of powerful engines. Because of the gentle rolling of the surface upon which he lay, he decided that he was aboard an airplane, flying through the night

Or was it day outside?

He brought his hands up to the top of his head, and tried to find an opening in the bag. Finally he did penetrate the point where the slip ropes were tied. He probed and tore at the hole with his powerful fingers and finally succeeded in making a one-inch gap at the opening.

Then he found the knot outside, twisted at it, and untied it. In moments he was drawing the sack down around his neck and shoulders, glancing about to see if anyone was watching.

The place he had been thrown was deserted. Crates and packages were stacked along the sides of what appeared to be a storage hold. Now the Phantom could clearly distinguish the hum of airplane engines. And he could see the dark sky through a small porthole.

He stepped out of the laundry bag, removed Prince Tydore's robe and turban, and made a quick reconnaissance of the plane. He was in the cargo hold of a freight transport. It was without passenger seats.

The Phantom could distinguish at least two men, and perhaps a third, in the cockpit. He recognized Baldy's gleaming skull. He did not recognize the other man; he seemed to have a very small head on a very large body.

After a few calisthenics, deep breathing, and some yoga relaxation exercises, the Phantom felt rejuvenated. He climbed back into the laundry bag and re-knotted the ropes.

He did not know how long he would have to wait for the plane to reach its destination, but he felt much better attired only in his skintight costume, hood, mask—and his weapons.

"It's a lot of trouble to go to," the Phantom said to himself. "But it's worth it, if I'm finally going to find out where they're keeping Diana."

It was daylight on the tropical beach where Sheik-al-Jabal Hara Kali stood peering into the sky. The radio message had been loud and clear: Prince Tydore had been seized and was being conveyed to the island.

Where was the plane?

Kali glanced impatiently at his wristwatch once again, pulling the sleeve of his crimson robe back to see the face. According to his calculations, the ship should be in sight now. Had something unforeseen happened?

He paced the small dock leading out into the bay. Those fools he had working for him in America had panicked once too often over some foolish, imagined Phantom! They would simply have to be replaced. It did not do for an Assassin to fear a ghost.

He lifted his head.

Was that the sound of an engine in the sky?

He squinted against the light, adjusting the monocle in his right eye, frowning slightly.

Yes!

The plane was coming into sight. Instantly, he felt exulted, elated and confident, for the first time in many hours. It seemed that almost everything that could go wrong had gone wrong with this series of operations.

First the interference with Diana Palmer's ransom. Then the abortive kidnap attempt on Princess Naji. And the Prince's ransom. But now, finally, Kali had Prince Tydore where he wanted him. He could ransom him for more than the ten million dollars he had originally intended. Maybe twenty million dollars. Maybe more!

Kali was rubbing his hands with glee.

Then, with the money, he could mount that scintillating attack on the American government, the attack that would divert all the riches of that country into the coffers of the Assassins. Then Kali could make the power play that would eventually take over the world!

The amphibian grew larger, its shape now quite distinct against the hot white sky.

As the ship lowered and curved in for a landing in the bay, its pontoons were gleaming in sunlight reflected from the water.

Hands clasped behind his robe, Kali moved to the end of the dock and watched. From behind him, he could hear the footsteps of several of his followers, dressed as he was in crimson robe and turban—the blood-red costume of the Cult of the Silken Noose.

The plane skipped down onto the water, throwing jets of foam high into the air, then slowly settled down into the bay. With the propellers idling, the ship coasted over toward the dock, rocking gently.

Kali caught the line and looped it around a stanchion. Through the cockpit window, he could see his men, grinning out at him. Ibn Saud, with his bald pate. Abu Fantu, with that short haircut. And Jamal Ingrin, the third member of the trio.

The crewmen climbed out of the ship and hopped to the dock.

"We've got him!" Ibn's bald head was gleaming with perspiration. "It was a breeze!"

Kali waved his hand irritably. "Let me see him."

Abu and Ibn ran to the side of the fuselage and quickly undid the snap locks on the loading port. The side lowered to the dock, and Kali could see inside the hold.

A large green bag lay tied in the middle of the deck.

"Laundry bag, Sheik Kali," said Ibn with a grin. "Nobody saw us take him out of the-hotel."

"Let him out." Kali's hands were trembling with eagerness.

Abu jumped into the hold and lifted the bundle by the armpits.

"He's plenty heavy for an old man," he laughed, rolling the sack out toward Ibn.

"Don't worry," Kali said, "he'll lose some weight in that cell we've got waiting for him."

The two men lowered the laundry bag to the dock. Kali stood over the bundle in eager anticipation.

"Open it up. I want to take a look at this man who means so many millions to me." He couldn't help gloating just a bit. It was all coming into focus, finally, after the many years of planning.

Ibn nodded and untied the knot, pulling the mouth of the opening wide.

Instantly the entire laundry bag shook, trembled, and dropped to the dock.

Out stepped a man dressed in skintight costume, with mask, with holstered weapons, and with a well-muscled body bursting forth from the garment.

"The Phantom!" croaked Ibn, his eyes rolling up into his head.

Angrily Kali backed off. "You bungling fools! Is this your nemesis?"

"But, Kali," whined Ibn in a strangled voice. "I don't know how—"

"So you are Kali," said the Phantom with a smile. "It's about time we met face to face."

"Seize him!" shouted Kali, motioning to the men who stood with him on the dock—men armed with knives and pistols. "Kill him!"

With drawn knives, the Assassins leaped on the Phantom

en masse. There was a flailing of fists and a chorus of grunts and groans. One Assassin fired a shot. The Phantom was bowled over backward. He twisted, cried out, and slipped into the water.

Kali folded his arms in satisfaction.

"Finish him off," he ordered.

Three Assassins dove in, knives drawn.

The water boiled and seethed.

It turned red.

Kali stroked his mustache. "Well, Ibn," he told the bald man, his monocle glinting. "That's the end of your Phantom."

CHAPTER 20

The bars of the cell windows were quite high, but Diana Palmer could see out if she dragged the chair over next to the wall and climbed up on it. There had been a great commotion outside, but Diana could not tell what had happened because she could not see anything but the courtyard outside the cell window.

She had heard the sound of the plane, and shortly after that, shouts and cries from the beach. Then there had been a great deal of running around outside the castle.

Then silence.

Now Diana listened to the footsteps of someone walking down the corridor toward her cell. The rhythm of the steps and the force with which they struck the paving blocks told her they were Kali's.

Suddenly the cell door jiggled and a key turned in the lock. Kali stood there, resplendent in his crimson robe.

"Come in here," Kali said to the man with him—a man in turban and loincloth, the work dress she had come to associate with Kali's followers.

Diana stood up, watching the red-robed tyrant. His normally imperturbable exterior was somehow ruffled.

"Has my ransom been paid?" Diana asked eagerly.

Kali's eyes narrowed. The monocle flashed with reflected

light. "I'm not here to discuss that, my dear."

"Then what is it?" Diana asked as insolently as she could.

Kali gazed at her briefly and turned to grasp the Assassin's naked arm. "Come here, Musa."

The heavy-featured Assassin complied without a word. He stood in front of Diana.

"Look at that man's jaw," Kali said slowly. "Does that mark mean anything to you?"

Diana studied the heavy-set man's face carefully. Musa was deeply tanned, his flesh as tough as leather. However, near the left side of his mouth a red bruise stood out fairly clearly. Diana's heart began pounding.

It was the Sign of the Skull! The imprint had come from the Phantom's ring!

Diana knew that the Phantom had come to the island to save her.

"The Phantom!" she gasped involuntarily.

Kali frowned. He pulled Musa aside and pushed him toward the cell door. "That's all. Get out."

Diana backed away, her heart fluttering in her throat.

Kali watched her narrowly. "Then you do know him."

"Yes," Diana admitted. "And he's here. I knew he would try to save me." She could not contain her exultation.

Kali began pacing. "My men are terrified of this person. They refuse to stand their guard shifts because of his presence." He cursed. "How much do you know about him?"

"His name is Kit Walker," said Diana. "He can do anything in the world. Some consider him a ghost. Others consider him a saint."

"But he's just a man, isn't he?" Kali's eyes were betraying uncertainty.

"He's a miracle worker," Diana contradicted.

Kali slapped a fist into his palm. "He's ruined my plans three times now. He's not going to ruin them again." Kali turned on her. "We killed him, you know." His eyes brightened with triumph.

"No!" gasped Diana.

"In the sea. Just now. He assumed the identity of one of my kidnap victims and was flown here. And he was fool enough to identify himself in front of me and my men. They dove into the water after him and cut him to ribbons." Kali was watching Diana.

"I can't believe it," wailed Diana.

"I wanted to be sure that he was the Phantom and that you knew him before I assured you he was dead," Kali gloated.

"How did it—how did it happen?"

"When he stepped out on the dock in his uniform, my men

attacked him with knives. They slashed him and he fell into the water. They followed, killing him." Kali paused and watched Diana's face.

"What did you do with him?" Diana's eyes were filled with tears.

Kali's eyes glinted. "His body drifted out to sea. We think the sharks finally got him."

"You didn't find his body?" Diana's spirits rose.

"No," Kali admitted. "My men are stupidly superstitious. They attribute superhuman powers to this man. But he's dead, I can assure you of that, Miss Palmer. You know he's no spirit from the other world!"

Diana concealed her elation. "He's a real man," she said.

"Real men are no match for my people," Kali said. "With the Phantom out of the way, I can once more open negotiations for your ransom, Miss Palmer, and finally kidnap Prince Tydore."

"You're a despicable man, Mr. Kali!" cried Diana, letting anger disguise her inner hope that the Phantom was alive and would save her. "Get out of my cell!"

Kali sneered. "You're completely at my mercy now, my dear. I wouldn't be so sassy if I were you."

Sheik-al-Jabal Hara Kali prowled the corridors of the Crusader castle with his hands clasped behind him, his monocle reflecting the stray rays of sunlight that crept into the dank interior through the high archery slits.

"My men aren't all that stupid," he muttered to himself. "I've pretended to them I never heard of this Phantom, but of course I misled them deliberately. Now, with that bruise on Musa's jaw, I know the truth for sure. The man who has been thwarting my every move is the Phantom."

Kali fumbled in his robe for his cigarette holder and lighter. In a moment he was puffing furiously on his ivory filter.

"It was he who attacked my men on the North Bridge and shot up my transmitter. It was he who attacked Ibn in Prince Tydore's car and kept us from taking Princess Naji. It was he who sent the pillowcase full of trinkets and books to the roof of the hotel. And it was he who impersonated Prince Tydore."

Kali cursed. "What happened to his body? Where is it? Maybe Ibn is right. Maybe he can walk on the bottom of the ocean! I couldn't tell Diana Palmer the truth—that my men were killed underwater, that the Phantom vanished. Nor can I admit to my men that I too believe in the Phantom's immortality!"

He rubbed his chin in frustration.

"If he's a man, he's indestructible! If he's a ghost, there's no way I can fight him. I have a problem of morale on my hands. How many of my men would stick by me if they knew I feared the Phantom more than anything else in the world?"

Kali snorted.

"They'll never know."

He paced the dank corridors of the dungeon wing. As he passed by one of the embrasures, he glanced out and saw the courtyard where Toto was chained.

His eyes lighted up.

"Toto! He's my answer to the Phantom. If the Phantom lives and is on the island, Toto can smell him out and kill him."

Kali puffed gleefully on his cigarette, watching the clouds roll up toward the damp ceiling.

"Toto has been trained from birth to kill anything that moves and is not impregnated with the smell of the Cult of the Silken Noose. When he sniffs out the Phantom, he'll tear him limb from limb."

Kali's eyes narrowed. "If, that is, the Phantom is flesh and blood and not thin air."

He laughed.

"Toto, at least, is not afraid of ghosts."

He hastened out of the dank corridor and called to his men. "Release Toto!"

With ease, the Phantom had dived backward into the shallow water at the side of the dock, avoiding the blows of the Assassins who had surged forward on Kali's command.

Quickly reversing his body, he jackknifed under and turned away from the point where he had entered the water. Immediately the surf was churned with the frenzied splashing of three Assassins coming after him.

The Phantom peeled away, watching them with amusement. He saw one grab another and stab at him repeatedly, the second releasing bubbles and screams simultaneously. Then the second went limp and sank to the sand below.

Number three turned away from the melee and saw the Phantom swimming to one side. He came immediately, knife stuck between his teeth. The Phantom waited, feigning inactivity, and the moment the third Assassin pulled the knife from his mouth and flung it at him, the Phantom reached for his own blade, raised it, and swiftly chopped at the Assassin from below.

Blood spurted out into the seawater.

The Assassin grabbed at the Phantom's hand, trying to wrest the blade out of it. The Phantom gripped hard on the Assassin's neck from behind, and the man went limp, sinking to the sand below.

The first Assassin had realized his error now and was swimming toward the Phantom with his own knife waving in front of him.

The Phantom dove to the bottom, lifted the dying man, raised him up to hurl him at the approaching Assassin.

Realizing the corpse was one of his companions, the killer with the knife backed off and swam around it to attack the Phantom from the other side.

Grasping the wrist of the attacker, the Phantom removed the knife without trouble and sliced the Assassin's chest. The Assassin shrieked and swam upward for the surface, streaming blood.

The Phantom quickly swam out of sight and hid under the shadow of the amphibian that bobbed up and down in the water.

With his sharp hearing, the Phantom could make out the muted conversation on the dock: Kali growling orders to his men, and his men refusing to go into the water to look for the Phantom.

Now one of the men found the bruise placed on his jaw by the Phantom's ring in the first assault. Kali studied it, but scoffed at its significance. The Assassins argued with their leader, and finally Kali ordered two men into the water to find the Phantom's body.

One by one the Assassins found the corpses of their companions.

Finally Kali left the dock, cursing at his men and berating them for their cowardice.

Soon there was no one left.

The Phantom swam a great distance underwater and finally surfaced in the waves around the rocks below the large stone promontory atop which sat the Crusader castle. The Phantom, in his moments on the dock, had immediately seen and memorized everything within sight and had categorized the large fortress as the living quarters and defense position of Kali. It would just as obviously be the place where he had imprisoned Diana Palmer.

With the entire coastline deserted and the air quiet except for the screeching of the inevitable seagulls, the Phantom climbed out of the water and crouched on the black rocks while the surf pounded at them. There he waited for twilight, which was not long in coming.

From the rocks he began climbing upward along the cliff toward the pathway that connected the beach with the castle.

Once on the path, he gained the courtyard. Fascinated by the structure that loomed up over him in the gathering darkness, the Phantom gazed at it with appreciation of its architectural solidity and its ancient design. He was also fascinated by the courtyard in which he found himself.

There was a high wall with cocopalms and tropical growth

in the corners. The courtyard itself was empty. Flagstones paved its surface.

A rusted chain hung loosely from the outer wall facing the sea. The Phantom studied it. He could see that although the chain was rusted, it showed rubbing and recent use.

Interesting.

As the Phantom paused to get his bearings, he turned to study the castle again. He was standing outside a tower that rose high in the air, with a crenelated design at the top and small window slits built in at intervals.

A nearby lower window was not six feet above the ground. It was barred. Light flickered from a candle or oil lamp inside. As he stared at the aperture, he wondered if it might not be the window of some prison cell, one Diana Palmer might be in.

He climbed to the bars, peering into the interior.

There was a candle burning on a table. He could see a shadowy form moving about in a stone-walled cell. It was a woman.

"Diana!" he cried.

She turned, her hand to her mouth in shock.

"Shh!" he cautioned. "Don't scream! It's me! I'm glad you're all right."

"Oh, yes," she sighed, climbing up on the chair and grasping the bars. "You're really here!"

"You bet your life I am."

"I knew you'd find me. This is a dreadful place."

The Phantom gave a sudden painful gasp.

"What's the matter?"

"Somethings got hold of my ankle," the Phantom said.

A grip stronger than any man's had hold of him, and as the Phantom turned to see what had grabbed him, a force that he could not withstand tore him away from the bars of the window and hurled him to the ground.

"Where are you?" Diana cried out.

The Phantom was on the flagstones, staring up in the moonlight at the ugliest gorilla he had ever laid eyes on. The gorilla was holding onto one leg. The beast growled throatily and started to pull at the Phantom's body.

CHAPTER 21

"It's Toto!" screamed Diana Palmer in her cell. "He's a killer. Kali must have turned him loose to hunt you down."

Now the Phantom understood the meaning of the huge chain hanging from the courtyard wall. That was Toto's leash.

With a quick twist and turn, the Phantom pulled himself loose from the grip of the gorilla and jumped to his feet, but the big beast immediately leaped at him again, letting out a loud roar of triumph.

The Phantom feinted toward the gorilla, turned, and lashed out at the chin of the beast with his rock-hard fist. The gorilla, unused to boxing tactics, had plunged straight toward the Phantom.

"Whew!" cried the Phantom, feeling the impact of the blow down to his toes. "This hurts me as much as it hurts you!"

Toto staggered back, raising his hands to his face and howling loudly at the pain in his head.

The Phantom drew up, glancing around hurriedly. "I can't use my guns or I'll bring all the Assassins on the island down on me."

Flight was the only answer.

The Phantom leaped past the still-dazed gorilla and bounded toward the pathway cut into the rock promontory. Toto growled, jumped up and down, and took off after the Phantom.

Quickly the Phantom fled down the trail, keeping his head

half turned to study the progress of the gorilla. He saw the beast swing up onto the courtyard wall and scramble down the steep side of the cliff, narrowing the distance between the two of them perceptibly.

The Phantom gained the beach and ran along it toward the dock. If he could get into the hydroplane, perhaps . . .

The hydroplane had been moved; the Phantom knew not where.

He turned to find some other avenue of escape, but could only see the slobbering beast loping after him. Then his foot caught in a coil of rope on the sand, and he fell to his knees. When he looked up, Toto was standing five feet away from him, glowering with those insane red eyes and making threatening sounds in his throat.

The Phantom reached down, never taking his eyes off the beast's, and picked up the coil of rope.

At the same instant, Toto shuddered and straightened again, growling with anger as he leaped at the Phantom. He struck the Phantom in the chest, and the Phantom went over backwards onto the sand, clutching the rope in his hand.

Toto leaped again.

The Phantom kicked up both feet at the beast's chest. Toto smashed into the Phantom's legs, and the impact knocked the breath out of the gorilla.

Gasping and beating his chest in agony, the great beast staggered backward and let out another howl of rage. Quickly the Phantom turned and flicked the rope, making a lasso out of it.

Toto was crouching now, staring at the Phantom, watching him with curiosity. The gorilla began lumbering forward, huge hands clenching and unclenching. Saliva dripped from the corners of its mouth. It was growling deep in its throat.

"I'll only get one try," the Phantom told himself as he twirled the lasso over his shoulder and let it fly toward Toto's head.

Toto rushed in, red eyes blinking rapidly. The noose of the lasso settled over the beast's head and dropped down around its shoulders.

"Made it," gasped the Phantom.

Toto stopped. As the Phantom tightened the rope, the noose held tightly to the beast's upper body. Quickly the Phantom picked up the remaining coil of rope and glanced hurriedly around. He had seen a tree with a thick lower branch some fifteen feet from the ground growing near the bottom of the embankment.

Toto roared in outrage and tried to slither out of the imprisoning rope. The beast had forgotten the Phantom's presence as this personal insult to its body baffled its tiny brain.

It growled menacingly, reaching up to tear the rope in two. But the rope held its limbs so close to its body that it could not budge.

It leaped up and down, stamping its feet on the sand.

The Phantom hurled the coil high into the air and over the bottom branch of the tree, letting it fall to the other side. Quickly he moved under the branch and began pulling the rope so that the line was now snugged against the gorilla, drawing the beast toward the tree.

Toto was fighting, snorting in puzzlement, kicking at the rope, and slobbering on the sand. The gorilla had now succeeded in drawing its limbs out of the noose, but as a result of that, the noose had settled around its trunk. As the Phantom pulled, the lasso settled around the upper chest of the beast, just under its armpits.

The beast roared in outrage and began shambling toward the Phantom.

"If the beast moves away from me, its weight can pull me into the air," the Phantom observed, holding tightly to the rope and searching around desperately for something to snag the rope to.

Toto bellowed and pounded his chest, moving toward the figure of the Phantom.

The Phantom said to himself, "It's like holding a tiger by the tail—you can't let go."

It was at that moment that the Phantom saw the large oil drum on the end of the dock. Quickly he ran to it and tied the line tightly to its middle.

He tried to push the drum over the edge into the water, but it was too heavy to budge.

Toto came toward him in the darkness, growling, arms extended toward the Phantom. At that moment, the rope drew tight around its chest and held it frozen in place. Toto roared and beat at the rope.

"If it figures out how to loosen that noose, I'm a dead man," thought the Phantom, struggling with the heavy oil drum. Then, suddenly, the Phantom remembered he had more strength in his legs than in his arms. He lay down on the dock, doubled up, and kicked out at the drum with his feet.

The drum toppled over into the water with a dull splash. The rope tightened, the weight of the drum pulled the line and snatched the big gorilla up off the ground, holding it suspended in the air just below the branch. The sound of howling and screaming filled the night.

Kali was at dinner when he heard the first of the roars.

"It's Toto!" he cried, standing up. "Ibn! Abu! Jamal!" He waited for his men to assemble. "Hurry up. I sent Toto out for the Phantom. I think the beast has tracked him down."

"Yes, sire," said Ibn.

"Bring guns and lights. I want my men to see that this Phantom is only a man like them."

They ran out into the night.

"There," Kali exulted, "listen to those screams. He's got the Phantom cornered."

Ibn said, "It's time something rotten happened to the Phantom."

"Down by the docks," Kali directed as they ran down the steep path cut into the rocky cliff.

They came out on a patch of sand in the moonlight, and for a moment Kali could not make out the scene at all.

"What's happened?" he cried out.

Ibn's bald head gleamed in the moonlight. He turned to his master with sardonic eyes. 'Toto! Helpless as a baby! High in the sky!"

Now Kali could see the giant gorilla, strung up by a rope to the branch of a high tree.

"Who did that?" Kali cried aloud.

Ibn chuckled ironically. "No man could!"

"Only a ghost," muttered Abu. "Or a Phantom!"

Kali ground his teeth in frustration. "All right, you idiots. Get the cage and lower the beast into it. I've had enough of this."

Ibn and Abu ran over to the tree while Jamal summoned help to drag out the cage on wheels from the storeroom of the castle. It took them fifteen minutes Jo cut the rope and lower the struggling gorilla into the cage and lock it up.

Then they hauled the sullen beast up the winding pathway back to the courtyard.

Kali peered in the cage and shone a flashlight on the gorilla.

Ibn let out a cry of astonishment. "Look!"

Kali leaned closer. The bald man was pointing at the collar around the gorilla's neck. Imprinted on its metallic surface was a familiar design: the death's head.

"The sign of the Phantom!" cried Jamal in terror.

"It was the Phantom!" said Abu in horror.

"The Phantom is not a man. He is the Ghost Who Walks." Jamal's teeth were chattering.

"He has the strength of ten tigers," Ibn muttered, a disbeliever convinced.

"Search the grounds for him," snapped Kali, realizing that his men were beginning to succumb to panic.

"Yes, yes," muttered Jamal, turning to flee into the shadows. Ibn followed.

"Come back, come back," shouted Kali. "Fools! He's only a man."

In the radio shack by the Crusader castle, the Assassin on duty awoke with a start and began jotting down the letters of the code he was listening to on the headphones. Although many messages were broadcast with voice transmissions, others were sent in code.

The operator knew that this code message had been posted by Agent Samson, who was stationed in a country near the island. Agent Samson was one of Kali's men who had been planted there some months before.

The radio operator quickly decoded the message and held it in his hands, studying it. Then he folded it up, stuck it in his belt, and ran out of the shack.

He found a sullen and frustrated Kali pacing beside his unfinished dinner in the refectory, muttering to himself and gnashing his teeth.

"Urgent message, sire!" said the radio operator.

Kali glared at him. He took the note and read it. Immediately his face cleared.

"So, Prince Tydore has left the United States and returned to Tydia. That means he's not far from us now. I think the Prince hasn't really escaped us yet."

"Yes, sire."

Kali smiled at the radio operator. "As soon as I dispose of the Phantom, I'll take care of the Tydore business. Things are looking up, Hassan."

"Yes, sire," said Hassan.

"Back to your transceiver, man," snapped Kali.

"Yes, sire."

Hassan hurried out of the castle and crossed the bare ground outside between the castle and the radio shack. The shack was built at the very highest point of the rock promontory.

The Phantom watched with amusement as Kali and his men arrived to observe Toto swinging in the air and bellowing with anger. He had swum away from the dock and once again made for the steep cliff upon which the castle was built.

He wanted to get back quickly to Diana's prison cell so he could try to work out some way to free her.

It was not to be—just yet.

As he made for the courtyard, he could hear three Assassins running toward him in the darkness. He hid behind a part of the courtyard wall, hanging down over the cliffside out of sight.

When the three men had left, he climbed up once again, only to hear Kali huffing and puffing across the courtyard with Baldy, Crewcut, and another man.

As he moved out of the shadows to follow them to the castle, the Phantom saw a slit of light appear quite abruptly in the darkness on the rock promontory past the castle.

His eyes instantly focused on a tiny cottage or hut built far away from everything else. The light inside the hut momentarily revealed a radio transmitter and tuner. The hut was, he realized instantly, the radio shack, the communications center. Oddly enough, the man went around the side of the castle and entered one of the doors leading to the room in which Kali and his men were standing.

The Phantom crouched outside the window and could see Kali clearly.

He heard the words he spoke to the radio man, whose name was Hassan. He heard Hassan's answers.

"Hmm," mused the Phantom. "So Prince Tydore is nearby, is he? That means that Tydia is not far from the island. I have no idea really where we are. But if Tydia is close, I can find out exactly where it is and I can figure out where we are."

As Hassan hurried from the castle door up the rocky walk to the communications shack, the Phantom followed quietly, keeping himself in the shadows of the rocks.

When Hassan had entered the radio room and shut the door behind him, the Phantom crept up to the window and peered in. Now he could see not only the transmitters, but a map on the wall showing a section of the continent and a dozen islands nearby. One of them must be the island of the Assassins.

He moved to the door and opened it silently.

Hassan felt the movement and turned to stare at him in astonishment that turned to abject fear.

The Phantom said, "Don't make a sound."

Hassan's voice gurgled in his throat. His eyes widened.

The Phantom smiled at his shock and started to move forward.

At that instant the muzzle of a gun barrel pressed into the Phantom's right temple. "Don't move, or I'll kill you," a voice said.

The Phantom turned his eyes slowly.

He saw Baldy grinning at him from the side, his eyes beady in the flickering light of the radio shack.

CHAPTER 22

The Phantom assessed the situation instantly. He knew that Baldy had made the cardinal error in close-range fighting tactics. By holding the barrel of the weapon in his hand against the Phantom's temple, he obviously hoped to frighten the Phantom into submission.

At the same time, however, he put himself within range of the Phantom's own potential counterattack. Had he covered the Phantom from ten paces away, he could easily have forced the Phantom to do as he wished, still having time to fire and stop him if he attacked.

By remaining within range of the Phantom's counterattack, he put himself in mortal danger.

Instantly, the Phantom's right elbow swung high in the air, slamming up against the underpart of Baldy's right arm. At the same moment, the Phantom pulled his head away from the gun barrel by swinging his neck and shoulders to the left and down. Simultaneously, his right hip smashed up into Baldy's midsection, and his right leg kicked around to knock the man's legs out from under him.

The gun fired, the slug tearing a hole in the ceiling of the flimsily constructed shack. The Phantom felt powder burns on his flesh, but he had pulled far enough away so that the shot did not do any serious harm. The echo of the shot reverberated in the confines of the room.

Hassan jumped up and stood frozen.

The Phantom leaped aside as Baldy rolled forward, slamming his head against the wall. The weapon fell from his limp hand. Quickly the Phantom reached for it and held it steadily on Hassan.

"That shot will rouse them, and they'll be here in moments. Quick, or I'll end your life instantly. Show me Kali's island on that map."

Hassan blinked and paled.

The Phantom moved quickly, gripping Hassan's neck at a pressure point.

Hassan grimaced.

"I don't like to hurt people, but with you, it's a pleasure. More, Hassan?"

"I—I—" Hassan felt the grip tightening and waved a hand toward the map. "There."

The Phantom glanced at the map. He could see the island that Hassan indicated. Near it he could make out a land mass.

"And that's Tydia?"

"Yesss," hissed Hassan.

"The call letters of Radio Tydia—quick!"

"T678," gasped Hassan.

The Phantom tightened his grip on the pressure point. "Thanks."

Hassan's eyes turned up in his head, and he sank to the floor to lie quietly beside Baldy.

Hastily the Phantom sat down in front of the controls, set the transmitter band, and called out the correct letters. He kept his eyes on the doorway, peering out into the night, waiting for the Assassins to come running in response to the shot fired.

"Calling T678," he said.

He was answered immediately.

"I can only say this once," the Phantom responded. "Pay attention! The message is for Prince Tydore, from Mr. Walker. I am on the island of the Assassins, located forty-seven miles on a course of one-six-eight from your capital. Mayday. Mayday."

The Phantom switched off the transmitter, rose from the seat, and ran out through the open door.

Already he could hear the steady pounding of running feet as the first of the Assassins rushed into the radio shack and cried out in shock at the sight of the two men on the floor.

"Get Jabal Kali! Ibn and Hassan are injured!"

Adjoining the dungeon chambers of the Crusader castle and the prison cells were the torture chambers used by the ancients to extract information from their enemies and to dispatch them to eternity.

Past the torture chambers was a large room with a low ceiling that extended into the gloom of the underground world below the castle. This was the room of Seva, the goddess of the Assassins. In the middle of the room stood a large idol constructed to conform to both the human and divine attributes of the goddess.

The face of the idol was round and fat, attached to a thin body that ended in a pedestal of sandstone. The sandstone surface was splotched with blood collected from centuries of sacrifices. In front of the pedestal lay a stone death couch equipped with leather straps and chains to secure recalcitrant sacrificial victims.

The idol's face was a grinning bulgy-eyed gargoyle of horror, but the body itself was an instrument of death and destruction. The goddess Seva was a many-armed deity, symbolizing the "many arms" of the Assassins who worshiped her. Each arm was extended like the spoke of a wheel, with a sharp knife clenched in the fist. The many arms of Seva were mounted on a wheel that rotated mechanically and was controlled by a switch concealed in the idol's body at the rear.

The knives rotated harmlessly as the wheel turned slowly—all but one.

That one arm extended out from the others, plunging downward onto the death couch in front of the idol. On this couch, a sacrificial victim could be secured by straps and chains until the machine within the goddess Seva's, body whirred and plunged the blade into the victim's heart.

Sheik-al-Jabal Hara Kali brooded in front of the ancient idol, touching his chin with his fingers, then slowly pacing back and forth.

"Bah! My men are errant fools," Kali said to himself. "They've allowed that man to wander all over the island—in the radio shack, on the dock, in the dungeons. It's a wonder he hasn't found Diana Palmer and freed her. But, of course, he would have to break into her cell to do that—and then where would he take her?"

Kali's eyes glittered.

"To stop him, I can't rely on my men anymore. I must flush him out myself."

Kali ceased his pacing, staring at the idol in the gloom before him.

"Seva! My goddess of murder! Just the one to help me find

this elusive, invisible Phantom!"

His voice echoed in the chamber.

"Ibn!"

Soon the bald-headed Assassin approached. His hairless head was now patched with a large bandage on the spot where he had been knocked unconscious in the radio shack.

"I come, sire."

"Get Diana Palmer."

Ibn's eyes widened. "I advise against that, Jabal Kali. The Phantom—he will know!"

"Yes," muttered Kali. "Get her, fool!"

Ibn inclined his head and left the chamber.

When he returned, he brought Diana Palmer with him. Diana's face was pale and shadowed. Kali approached one of the oil lamps in the wall and touched his cigarette lighter to it. The wick took flame and brightness poured from the lamp, casting enormous shadows in the room.

He turned to observe Diana.

She was a beautiful creature. Perhaps he should give up his idea of ransoming her, he thought, and take her as his queen.

"What do you want?" she snapped at him, her eyes terrified at the sight of the bloodstained idol.

"My dear, it is good to see you. I have been wondering how to make use of your presence here. Now I have finally decided."

"And how is that, Mr. Kali?" Diana asked sarcastically.

"In the old days we made living sacrifices here to this goddess of the many arms. I've been thinking of reviving the ancient custom."

Diana shuddered. "No! How can you?"

"Very easily, my dear. Ibn! Seize her and strap her to the sacrificial couch!"

The bald-headed Assassin bowed and grasped Diana by the arms. She screamed and jabbed her elbows into his stomach, but he lugged her grimly toward the stone idol and threw her down on the couch, then quickly grabbed the straps, thrust her wrists through the loops and tightened the cinches.

"Don't do this to me!" cried Diana. "You'll never get your ransom money now!"

Kali smirked. "Won't I? Who'll know?"

Ibn thrust Diana's ankles through the leg straps and pulled the cinches tightly. Diana gasped and struggled against the grip of the leather thongs. She only succeeded in twisting her blouse and skirt around her straining body.

"Doesn't she make a beautiful sight on the sacrificial couch?" gloated Kali. "Let us leave our goddess in solitude, fellow

Assassins. When we return, the victim will be destroyed."

He leaned over and pressed the hidden switch button behind the stone idol. The goddess Seva's many arms began their slow rotation.

Kali smiled at Diana and slowly walked through the gloom with his men.

"Help!" screamed Diana.

It was obvious to the Phantom where the activity in the castle was centered. He had followed the first of the Assassins into the darkened recesses of the dungeon chambers, the torture chambers, and then into the sacrificial room. By keeping to the outside of the castle, he could peer in through the narrow window slits and watch what went on inside.

He saw Kali brooding in front of the goddess Seva with her many-handed wheel of death; he heard Kali send for Diana; he saw them strap Diana to the sacrificial couch, turn on the machine and leave.

He saw the knife arm of the goddess Seva begin its slow revolution toward Diana's breast, and that was the moment he ran through the shadows, entered the sacrificial room from the side and pounded across the floor to the diabolical machine.

"Oh, darling!" gasped Diana. "Hurry!"

In moments, the Phantom had unstrapped Diana Palmer and held her in his arms. The descending knife plunged into the place where Diana's body had lain and the wheel stopped with a shudder.

"Look out!" cried Diana, pointing over the Phantom's shoulder.

The Phantom wheeled, still holding her. There stood Kali, with Baldy and Crewcut beside him. As the Phantom debated his next move, a group of six Assassins he had not seen grabbed him from behind, smothering him with the press of their bodies.

He went down.

Diana was snatched from him, screaming.

The Phantom lost consciousness as the pummeling fists of the Assassins smashed into his skull and body.

He revived to find himself flat on the sacrificial couch, his hands bound in leather thongs, his ankles trussed tightly.

He was not alone.

Kali stood above him, a cigarette slowly burning in the ivory holder, his monocle flashing in the flickering flames of the oil lamp in the wall niche.

"So," Kali mused. "You avoided all my traps until I used

the most irresistible bait in the world, eh?"

"Yes," snapped the Phantom, pulling at the thongs, which he knew were far sturdier than hempen ropes.

"You suspected this was a trap, is that right?" the gloating Kali continued.

"Yes."

"Yet you came," Kali chuckled. "How stupid of you. Shakespeare was wrong when he said, 'Men have died, but not of love.' You will!"

The Phantom smiled. "It's as good a reason as any."

Then in the shadows behind the leader of the Assassins, the Phantom saw Diana, crying morosely against the wall.

"Oh, Kit!" she wailed.

Kali flicked the ashes off his cigarette and turned to Diana. "You shall remain here while the goddess chooses to destroy your lover. Do you think you're worth all the trouble you've put this brave man to?"

"You're a beast," sobbed Diana. "A beast! No better than Toto!"

"Better than Toto," chortled Kali. "At least I have not been bamboozled by the Phantom." He sneered the word. "Phantom! He's just another man like the rest of us mortals."

"Not like the rest of you," Diana said defiantly.

"We'll see." Kali leaned down over the Phantom. "I sent out my men because I'm curious about you. Are you really four hundred years old? Are you the mythical Phantom?"

The Phantom smiled but said nothing.

"Your silence is deafening," said Kali, laughing at his own joke. "No matter. My only interest in you is to see you good and dead. At once!"

Diana came out of the shadows. "Mr. Kali! Don't do it. Please. I'll do anything to save him."

Kali turned to her scornfully. "No, my dear. You will do nothing to save him. The goddess wants his blood." Kali leaned over the back of the idol. "I press this button, the arms revolve, all missing you until the long arm reaches you. My followers are superstitious. You've terrorized them with your tricks. I must undo all that."

There was the sound of whirring and grumbling. Slowly the arms began to revolve on the wheel of death.

Diana Palmer burst into tears.

The knife slowly descended toward the Phantom's chest. He watched it, unable to move from the death couch. The point was inches from his chest.

"Have you anything to say?" Kali asked the Phantom.

"Yes! You Assassins are finished."

Kali chuckled. "What colossal nerve. If I didn't loathe you so much, I think I could almost admire your steel nerve."

The knife descended toward the Phantom's body and he tensed his muscles, unable to stop it. In a moment now, it would pierce his heart and . . .

CHAPTER 23

Watching the knife in Seva's mechanical arm move toward the chest of the Phantom, Sheik-al-Jabal Hara Kali leaned forward expectantly, his monocle almost slipping from his eye in his eagerness.

A jarring explosion ripped through the rock upon which the Crusader castle was built, making the ancient stone walls tremble and shake. There was sufficient force from the impact to throw Kali to the floor.

"What was that?" a voice shouted in the gloom.

"The Phantom is bringing the castle down around our ears!" Abu shrieked, and began running for the doorway.

"Fools!" Kali cried, rising and staring about him in rage and puzzlement. "Stay!"

At that moment another explosion rocked through the castle. The blast's epicenter seemed somewhat removed from the immediate area.

Kali sniffed the air, alert as a hunting dog. "Cordite! It's gunpowder."

A third explosion followed, this one nearer still. Now Kali was moving quickly toward the doorway of the sacrificial chamber, reaching up to adjust his monocle.

"It's an attack on the island," cried a disheveled Assassin

who rushed in toward Kali, waving his hands in the air. He seemed more than half crazed by fear.

"Stop, fool," snapped Kali. 'Tell me the facts."

"We're at war," shouted the Assassin. "Huge warships are in the harbor. Dive bombers. It's Armageddon."

Kali flinched, but held his ground. "Go back into the open, and tell my men to assemble at the rear of the castle. We'll repel the would-be invaders, if that's what they are. Ibn!" he shouted. Get to the artillery positions in the rock. Hurry! We're being invaded."

"Yes, sire." Ibn rushed out into the corridor.

"Who could have discovered our presence here?" Kali wondered aloud as he hastened through the darkened hallways toward the rear of the castle. "They'll learn how hard it is to dislodge warriors from a fortress rock."

From the shadows of the sacrificial chamber, Diana Palmer ran across the stone floor to the mechanical idol of the goddess Seva. The Phantom turned his head, watching her.

"Darling!" she cried. "How do I turn the infernal thing off?"

The Phantom shook his head. "I don't know, Diana. I saw Kali bend over behind the idol."

Diana was weeping during her frenzied attempts to shut the torture device off. She stumbled and finally came to the side of the pedestal.

"I can't find it!" she wailed, groping in the darkness for the switch.

"It's a button," the Phantom explained coolly.

The knife blade touched his chest; he could feel the pressure of the machine behind the blade.

"A button?"

The knife went into the Phantom's suit, cutting it, gashing the flesh.

"Yes," said the Phantom, gritting his teeth against the pain. He exhaled all the breath from his chest, bringing the level of his body down at least two inches.

The blade continued its inexorable movement.

"I don't—I can't—oh, my darling! I can't find it—I—"

The blade pierced the Phantom's chest just as the machine clanked to a stop.

"Is that it?" Diana asked in wonder, rising, her face streaked with tears.

"Yes!" The Phantom tried to roll out from under the blade, but could not. "Get me out of these straps!"

Diana tugged at the leather thongs, and once again there were explosions that shook the castle.

"What's happening out there?" Diana wondered.

"The island is being attacked by Prince Tydore's men," said the Phantom with a faint smile.

"Who is Prince Tydore?" Diana asked.

The Phantom pulled his wrists from the loosened straps and rolled out from under the knife, then leaned down and unfastened his ankles. He sat on the edge of the sacrificial couch rubbing his wrists and trying to restore circulation to his numbed limbs.

"It's a long story."

"But you're all right now!" Diana blinked back more tears.

"You've saved my life, Diana," said the Phantom gently. Then he jumped to his feet. "I've got to help the invaders smash the Assassins. You stay here where it's safe." The Phantom bolted for the door of the sacrificial chamber.

The shelling of the island began just before dawn, and the final shot was fired not two hours later. Elements of the French navy, patrolling the waters off Tydia, which had been a French protectorate, were able to blast out the gun batteries and smash every military position on the island by means of landing barges, armed marines, and air assault.

There was very little loss of life on either side. Kali's Assassins, though skilled in subterfuge, were not adept at open military fighting. They ran when the odds turned against them, no matter how persistently Kali tried to rally them to fight.

After the gun batteries were seized, spiked, or destroyed, the Assassins were hunted down, disarmed, tied up and removed to the brig of the fleet flagship. Kali was missing.

The Phantom brought Diana up into the sunlight, at which she blinked briefly until her eyes were accustomed to the brightness of day that her imprisonment had denied her.

"Darling," she said. "It's all over!"

"We haven't found Kali yet," said the Phantom.

At the height of the mop-up operations, the two of them met Prince Tydore accompanying his marines in the courtyard of the castle.

"There you are, Mr. Walker," Prince Tydore exclaimed upon seeing the Phantom.

The Phantom introduced Diana to Prince Tydore, briefly explaining about the attempted kidnapping of the Royal Princess and Royal Prince.

"Can you imagine?" Prince Tydore said. "This island is

under my domain, and the Assassins have been here all the time. That's why they chose me to extort money from. I'll destroy all traces of this infestation."

A marine officer rushed up. "We've found Kali, Your Highness," he reported. He explained that Kali had been captured at his post in the main gun batteries next to the Crusader castle after all his men had deserted him.

In a moment, the monocled crimson-robed fanatic was brought to stand before Prince Tydore and the Phantom.

"Ah, Your Highness," Kali muttered with a charming smile. "I heard how you hid in a closet while my men searched for you in the Royal Suite."

"Laugh while you can," snapped Prince Tydore.

"So you won after all," Kali acknowledged woodenly, glancing at the Phantom and then briefly at Diana. "Would you mind telling me how, for future reference?"

The Phantom stepped forward. "You have no future, Kali, You and your Assassins are finished."

"Hmph," sniffed Kali.

"Take him away," Prince Tydore ordered loftily. He turned to the Phantom. "And now that we are finished here—will you bring me my daughter?"

Diana Palmer turned to the Phantom. "His daughter?"

"The Princess Naji," said the Phantom. "She's at the Cave of Skulls."

Diana's face drained of color. "But—"

"Prince Tydore, would you take care of Miss Palmer while I get Princess Naji?"

"Certainly."

"I'll bring her to your palace." The Phantom turned to Diana. "Then I'll take you home to America."

On the flight from Bangalla to Tydia, the Phantom recounted the seizure of the island where Kali's kidnappers had hidden out, including his rescue of Diana Palmer.

"Who's she?" asked Princess Naji, watching the Phantom's face closely.

"Just a girl," said the Phantom.

When they landed at the airport near the capital of Tydia, a huge cavalcade of Tydian military escorted them to the palace. Princess Naji waved to her subjects with the Phantom at her side. Prince Tydore and his daughter were reunited in a gay and elaborate ceremony, which included the aged and bedridden king, her grandfather.

Suddenly, the Phantom found himself alone with Princess

Naji and Diana Palmer in a small chamber adjoining the throne room.

"Well?" said Diana Palmer, meaningfully.

"Well, what?" the Phantom mumbled. He didn't like the vibrations in the room.

"Introduce me," Diana demanded frostily.

The Phantom turned to Princess Naji. He was taken aback by the icy glint in her eyes as she surveyed Diana Palmer. It was odd. Everybody else liked Diana.

"Your Royal Highness, this is Diana Palmer," the Phantom said, feeling perspiration trickle off his forehead.

"Indeed," said Princess Naji distantly.

"And this is Princess Naji," said the Phantom.

Diana's face was carved out of stone. She was staring at the Princess of Tydia with blood-curdling hostility.

"Just a girl," remarked Princess Naji, glancing with scorn at the Phantom.

"I beg your pardon?" The Phantom could feel the Princess's indignation.

"She's very beautiful," said the Princess, forcing the words out.

"Of course," said the Phantom, baffled at the Princess's remarkable hostility.

"And she was in the Cave of Skulls?" Diana Palmer snapped bitingly at the Phantom, her eyes cutting Princess Naji like diamond on glass.

"Why, yes," said the Phantom, suddenly flustered. "Say, you don't think there was anything—uh, like that—going on, do you, Diana?"

"Like that?" Princess Naji's face was pale. "Does this woman have some strange hold on you, Mr. Walker?"

The Phantom took a deep breath. "Girls, please," he said, backing away. "If I'd known you were going to be at each other's throats this way, I never would have brought you together."

Diana turned on the Phantom. "Just why did you bring us together?"

Princess Naji frowned and turned on the Phantom. "I also await your answer."

The Phantom paled. "I thought you'd like each other. Two beautiful women, smart, sophisticated, intelligent—"

Simultaneously Princess Naji and Diana Palmer burst out laughing.

"What's the matter?" the Phantom asked innocently.

Diana Palmer struggled to stop laughing. "The great Phantom can do anything—except handle women."

"Especially beautiful women!" gasped Princess Naji with fits of mirth.

The Phantom flushed. "I didn't mean anything. I just wanted you to like each other."

The laughter ceased abruptly.

Princess Naji spoke softly. "Leave us alone for a few moments, Mr. Walker."

Diana Palmer nodded. "Yes. We'll settle this. It's really none of your business."

The Phantom protested. "But I don't know if you'll be safe with each other—"

They pushed him out of the room. The Phantom held his ear to the door panels, pondering the inscrutability and incomprehensibility of woman.

Two days later, the Phantom sat in the Cave of Skulls, still shaken by the encounter between Diana Palmer and Princess Naji.

Guran, the leader of the pygmies, sat at his feet, grinning with encouragement as he listened to the Phantom's narration.

"And whom did you choose?"

The Phantom blinked. "I chose neither, fool! I simply listened outside the door, wondering when I should rush in to separate them. After all, I was intelligent enough to realize that they were going to fight each other—over me!"

Guran nodded. "Yes. Go on."

"I couldn't hear a thing. I waited around. I cooled my heels at the Princess's door." The Phantom shook his head ruefully. "Nothing."

"But where is Diana Palmer now?" Guran asked.

"In Paris."

"And where is the Princess?"

"In Paris."

Guran half stood, his whole body shaking with anxiety. "O Ghost Who Walks, where is the bride of the Phantom?"

"There is no bride of the Phantom," said the Phantom with a suddenly relaxed grin. "The Princess and Diana developed such an excellent friendship—I knew they would like one another—that they're on a shopping spree in Paris and London."

"But—but—when is the Phantom bringing his bride to the Cave of Skulls?" sputtered Guran.

The Phantom leaned back, laced his fingers behind his head, and grinned at the ceiling.

"When the shopping money runs out," he answered. "And those two are the richest women in the world, I'm told."

Guran looked stricken.

The Phantom chuckled, softly at first, and then with increasingly less restraint.

COMING SOON FROM HERMES PRESS

Volume 15: THE CURSE OF THE TWO-HEADED BULL

THE PHANTOM AMBUSHED IN A SHEIK'S HAREM?

There was no immediate escape route. Without hesitation, he spread his arms so that they touched three or four girls on either side, and moved rapidly to the pool. A half dozen girls ahead were propelled with them as he jumped into the pool, pulling them all with him.

There was pandemonium in the harem as the others ran every which way screaming .... the amazed soldiers ran to the edge of the pool, trying to spot the big stranger whom they had glimpsed only briefly. He wasn't in sight. He was somewhere underwater, among the trashing bodies.